# Radiance

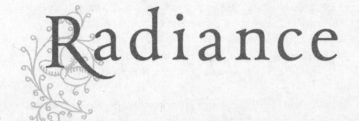

*a novel by*

# alyson noël

SQUARE
FISH

St. Martin's Griffin
New York

To Jean Feiwel, for making this possible—
thank you, thank you, thank you!

A SQUARE FISH BOOK
*An Imprint of Macmillan*

Library of Congress Cataloging-in-Publication Data

Noël, Alyson.
Radiance. Book 1 / Alyson Noël. — 1st ed.
p. cm.
Summary: After crossing the bridge into the afterlife, a place called Here where
the time is always Now, Riley's existence continues in much the same way as
when she was alive until she is given the job of Soul Catcher and, together
with her teacher Bodhi, returns to earth for her first assignment, a ghost called
the Radiant Boy who has been haunting an English castle for centuries and
resisted all previous attempts to get him across the bridge.
ISBN: 978-0-312-62917-5
[1. Future life—Fiction. 2. Ghosts—Fiction. 3. Dead—Fiction.] I. Title.
PZ7.N67185Rad 2010 [Fic]—dc22 2010015840

Cover photographs: bridge © Hiroshi Watanabe/Gallerystock; girl © Betsie
Van der Meer/Getty Images; dog © Radius Images/Jupiterimages;
field © plainpicture/Maskot

Square Fish logo designed by Filomena Tuosto

*Book design by Susan Walsh*

First Edition: 2010

10 9 8 7 6 5 4 3 2 1

www.squarefishbooks.com

*"I may be dead, but I'm still pretty."*

—buffy the vampire slayer

**M**ost people think that death is the end.
     The end of life—of good times—the end of, well,
pretty much everything.

But those people are wrong.

Dead wrong.

And I should know. I died almost a year ago.

2

The weirdest part about dying is that nothing really changed.

I mean, you'd expect a big change, right? Because dying—well, let's face it, it's pretty dramatic stuff. They write songs about it, books and screenplays too. Heck, it's even a major theme on Saturday morning cartoons. But the thing is, it's nothing like you see on TV.

Nothing at all.

Take me for instance. I'm living, er, make that *dead* proof that it really isn't so different. Or at least not at first. And at least not in a bad way like you probably think.

Because the truth is, the moment I died I actually felt more alive than ever. I could jump higher—run faster—I could even walk through walls if I wanted. And that's pretty much what gave it away.

The walking-through-walls part.

Since it's not like I could do that sort of thing before, so that's how I knew something was up.

Something serious.

But up until then, it all just seemed like a really cool side trip. Like my dad just decided to take a sudden turn none of us were expecting.

One moment he was cruising down a curving highway, while I was singing along to my iPod with my dog Buttercup resting his head on my lap, doing my best to tune out my bossy older sister Ever who practically lived to torment me. And the next thing I knew, we were somewhere else entirely.

No longer on the highway, no longer in Oregon, we'd somehow landed smack dab in the middle of this beautiful shimmering field full of pulsating trees and flowers that shivered. And when my parents went one way and my sister went another, I just stood there, head swiveling like crazy, unsure who to follow.

Part of me urging, "Cross the bridge with Mom and Dad and Buttercup—they know what's best!"

While the other part insisted, "Don't be such a goody-good—if Ever sees something awesome and you miss out, you'll regret it forever!"

And by the time I finally decided to go after my sister, I'd taken so long she was already gone.

Just—disappeared.

Straight into the shimmering mist.

Right back to the earth plane.

And that's how I ended up stuck. Stuck between worlds.

Until I found my way Here.

That's what they call it, "Here."

And if you're dumb enough to ask what time it is, they'll say, "Now."

Probably because there's no time Here, which means everything happens, well, in the moment it happens, which is always just—*Now*.

So, I guess you could say I live in the Here & Now.

Which, strangely, isn't so different from where I lived before back in Eugene, Oregon.

Aside from there being no time. And of course, that bit about being able to walk through walls and stuff.

But other than that, and the fact that I can manifest anything I want—stuff like houses and cars and clothes, even animals and beaches, simply by imagining it—it's all pretty much the same.

My parents are Here. My grandparents too. Even my sweet yellow Lab Buttercup made it. And even though we can live anywhere we could ever conceivably want, in any kind of house we could ever truly desire, the funny thing is that my new neighborhood is pretty much an exact replica of my old neighborhood back in Oregon.

Everything identical, all the way down to the clothes that hang in my closet, the socks that are stuffed in my drawers, and the posters that are taped to my walls. The only thing that's different, the only thing that kind of bugs me, is all the other houses around us are empty. Mostly due to the fact that all my old neighbors and friends are alive and well and back in the earth plane (well, for now anyway!). But still, other than that, it's exactly like I remember it.

Exactly like I wished it.

I just wish I had some friends to enjoy it with.

# 3

When I woke up this morning—oh, that's another thing—you probably thought I didn't need to sleep, right? Well, at first, that's what I thought too. But as my parents explained it to me, we are, in a sense, more alive than ever, made up of energy in its purest form. And after a long day of creating and manifesting and, well, whatever else people choose to do Here, the energy requires a little downtime, a little shut-eye, in order to rest, recuperate, and regenerate— which, again, is no different from life on the earth plane.

So anyway, when I woke up this morning with Buttercup wagging his tail and licking my face, despite the fact that it's a pretty nice way to wake, that didn't stop me from pushing him away, pulling the blanket over my head, and rolling over so that my back was facing him. My eyelids squinched together as tightly as they would go, and I tried to find my way back to my dream as Buttercup continued to whimper and whine and paw at me.

And just as I was about to push him away yet again, that's when I remembered:

Buttercup was excited for me.

Everyone was excited for me.

From the moment I got Here, I'd pretty much kept myself busy with getting adjusted to my new life, getting reacquainted with my family, and basically trying to learn how things are done in this place. And now that I was settled, it was time for my first day of school (yes, we have school Here—it's not all cloud lounging and harp playing, you know), and since everyone was acting so excited about it, it became my job to act excited too.

Excited enough to get out of bed, get myself ready, and take the time to manifest something cool to wear, so I could, well, according to my parents anyway, head off to a place where I'd:

*"Meet some new friends, learn some new things, and in no time at all find myself picking up right smack where I left off back home!"*

And no matter how much I doubted that, no matter how much I was willing to bet just about anything that there was no way that would turn out to be even remotely true, I just smiled and went along with it. Wanting them to think I was as eager for the moment as they clearly were.

Not wanting them to know just how much I missed my old life back home. Missed it so much it was like a constant ache in my middle. And how I was pretty dang sure that this school, no matter how cool they claimed it to be, could never compete with the one I'd left behind.

So after enjoying a little breakfast with my mom and dad (and no, we don't really need to eat anymore, but would you give up the taste of Lucky Charms if you didn't have to?), I set off. At first dressed in a typical private-school uniform of white blouse, plaid skirt, blue blazer, white socks, and cool shoes, since I always wanted to go to a school that required that, but then halfway there I changed my mind and swapped it for some skinny jeans, ballet flats, and a soft, fuzzy blue cardigan I wore over a white tank top featuring the logo of my favorite band.

Seriously, manifesting is really that easy—or at least it is Here. You just think of anything you want, anything at all, picture it really clearly in your head—*et voilà*—just like that, it's yours!

So anyway, I kept going like that, switching back and forth, forth and back, between the two looks. Taking two steps forward as a private-school girl, and another two dressed as an extremely stylish twelve-year-old girl. Figuring I'd stick with whatever ensemble I was wearing by the time I reached campus, knowing I could always change it in an instant if it turned out to be the wrong choice.

But then, somewhere along the way, I saw *it*.

The Viewing Room.

The place my parents had warned me about.

Insisting it would lead to no good. That I would only become obsessed yet again just when I needed to focus my energies on moving on, settling in, and accepting the fact that, like it or not, I am now an official resident of the Here & Now. Claiming it was high time I turn my back on my old life and concentrate on embracing my afterlife.

"You lingered on the earth plane long enough," my dad said, giving me his usual compassionate yet concerned look.

While my mom looked on, eyes narrowed, arms crossed, not fooled by my claims of mere mild curiosity for a second. "Your sister has her own lessons to learn, her own destiny to fulfill, and it's not your place to interfere," she'd said, refusing to budge or even try to see my side of things.

But even though their intentions were good, the thing is, they didn't know my sister nearly as well as I did. Didn't realize she needed me in a way they could never even begin to comprehend. Besides, if it's true that there's no time, then it's not like I could be late for school, right? So really, what's the worst that could happen?

With my mind fully made up, I took a little detour and ducked inside, snatching a ticket from the dispenser on the wall before taking my place in a very long line. Surrounded

by a whole gang of gray hairs gushing on and on about the grandkids they couldn't wait to look in on, until my number finally flashed on the overhead screen and I marched straight into the recently vacated cubicle, closed the curtain behind me, settled onto the hard, metal stool, and punched in my desired location, carefully scanning the screen until I found her.

Ever.

My sister.

My blond-haired, blue-eyed, teenaged sister who looks an awful lot like me except for our noses. She was lucky enough to get our mom's perfectly straight nose—while I got my dad's, *er*, stubbier one.

"A nose with character," my dad liked to say. "There's not another one like it, not anywhere—except on your face!" Always chasing it with one of those nostril tweaks that never failed to make me laugh.

But even though I watched for what felt like a pretty long time, I couldn't say I saw all that much. Or at least nothing important anyway. Nothing that could be considered heart stopping (and *no*, my heart doesn't really beat anymore, it's just a figure of speech). Basically what I saw was a girl just going through the motions, trying really hard to make everyone around her think she was a perfectly normal person, living a perfectly normal life, when the truth is, I knew for a fact that she was anything but.

Still, I couldn't stop looking. Couldn't stop that old feeling from overtaking me again.

The one where my heart felt as though it would swell so big I was sure it would burst wide-open and blow a big hole right through my chest.

The one where my throat went all hot and lumpy, where my eyes started to sting, and I was filled with such longing, such overwhelming yearning, I was willing to do anything to go back.

Back to the earth plane.

Back to where I truly belonged.

Because the truth is, as hard as I'd been trying to put on a brave face and make everyone think I was adjusting just fine and really learning to love my new life Here—the fact is, I wasn't.

I wasn't adjusting.

I wasn't learning to love much of anything.

Not. At. All.

In fact, given the opportunity, I would've done anything to locate that bridge again so I could sprint right across it without once looking back.

I'd do anything to go back home, to my *real* home, and live alongside my sister again.

And it didn't take a whole lot of screen time to know that Ever felt pretty much the same way. Because not only did she

miss me, it was pretty clear she needed me as much as I needed her.

And that's all I needed to go on to know I'd done the right thing.

That's all I needed to see to not feel the least bit bad for going against my parents' wishes and sneaking into the Viewing Room.

Because the truth is, I felt justified.

Sometimes you just have to act on your own.

Sometimes you have to do what you know inside to be right.

# 4

After watching for what seemed like a while, I gave up my stall to some middle-aged guy with one of those curlicue mustaches that you see way more in cartoons than real life, vacated the Viewing Room, and arrived at school dressed in the plaid skirt, white blouse, and blue blazer, and decided to just go with it barring some sort of major, catastrophic, fashion-related embarrassment.

Happy to see I wasn't the only one wearing a uniform, that plenty of other kids were wearing them too. Though there were also kids dressed in saris and kimonos and all sorts of really cool, international wear, with pretty much every ethnicity present and accounted for. And that's when it hit me—the full scope of what was really happening Here.

I was finally the exchange student I always wanted to be.

When the soft, tingling sound of wind chimes trilled through the air, everyone started heading in the same general direction, and since I had no idea what to do, or where I was expected to be, I followed.

Merging into the throng of students as we made our way down a beautifully landscaped path filled with all sorts of exotic flowers, plants, and trees, over a small bridge that spanned the biggest, most amazing koi pond I'd ever seen, and into some building that looked just like the pictures I'd seen of the Parthenon in Greece, except this one wasn't all old and crumbly with missing columns and stuff. This particular version was made of marble so shiny, white, and pristine it looked as though it had been built that very same day.

We made our way up the stairs and took our places on a long marble bench. Squeezing in next to a girl in a royal blue and bright yellow cheerleading uniform on one side, as a boy in a long beige cotton tunic, matching cotton pants, and old leather sandals squeezed in on my other. And I was just about to turn to him, eager to strike up a conversation and ask him where he was from and how long he'd been dead, when this old dude with long, sparkly, golden-colored hair (yes, it actually *sparkled*—I'm not making that up) in a long, shimmering robe that was so long it puddled around his feet and dragged on the floor behind him like a bridal train, sort of glided into the room as everyone rose from their seats.

Everyone but me, that is.

Because the thing is—seeing him standing there before us like that, well, I was a little taken aback.

Not to mention choked up.

I mean, even though I figured I'd been Here for probably what amounted to a week (I kept track of time by how many times I went to sleep, counting one for each day), I'd yet to see the Big Guy, otherwise known in these parts as The One.

But apparently I still hadn't, because cheerleader girl sitting next to me grabbed hold of my jacket and continued to yank on my sleeve until we were standing shoulder to shoulder, her mind hissing at mine: *What're ya doin', mate? You better stand up so Perseus can count you!*

"Perseus?" I looked at her, not realizing I'd spoken out loud until the dorky guy with the greasy hair and nerd glasses sitting right in front of me turned and thought: *Shhh!*

I clamped my lips shut and stared straight ahead, feeling as though that Perseus dude was looking right at me, but then, after gazing around a bit, I realized he was. But not just at me, he was pretty much looking at everyone, conducting a sort of mental roll call it seemed, which probably explained why everyone was on their best behavior.

Up until then, I'd never seen such a large group of well-behaved students, especially at an assembly like this. And I couldn't help but hope that wouldn't always be the case. That we didn't all just immediately turn into angels and saints by virtue of being Here. That somewhere in the crowd was at least one potential friend who'd understand the fundamental value of goofing off.

Because if not, well, how boring would that be?

And I was so lost in the thought I didn't even realize the music had started until cheerleader girl nudged me on the arm and pointed to where Perseus now stood center stage. An electric guitar strapped across his chest as he led us all in a rousing chorus of "You Can't Always Get What You Want." Dragging the song out for much longer than necessary, much longer than I remember it being, and even adding in some major guitar riffs I know for a fact I never heard on my dad's old CDs. Gladly accepting his standing ovation the moment it was finally, mercifully over, and promptly discarding his glittering robe and revealing himself to be just another old-school hippie in faded jeans, vintage Rolling Stones concert tee, and bare feet.

*You shoulda been 'ere last time when he made us sing "Get Off of My Cloud,"* cheerleader girl thought, pushing down on my shoulder, signaling that it was time to sit once again, and leaning toward me when she whispered, "It went on forever. I swear, he's just biding his time 'til Mick and Keith show up, then we'll never see 'im again." And when she pulled away, she smiled so brightly it made her whole body radiate with the most wonderful green-tinged glow.

"How'd you do that?" I asked, ignoring whatever tele-pathic message Perseus was now sending in favor of taking in her long rows of braids with the beautiful, multicolored beads dangling from the ends, her large, brown eyes, full pink lips, and dark skin. Seeing the question in her gaze, the way her head cocked to the side, and further explaining when I thought: *You know, glow like that? How'd you do it?*

She looked at me, eyes narrowed as she took her time taking me in. Starting at my shoes and slowly working her way up to my bangs that were brushed to the side in the way I'd recently started experimenting with. Seemingly just about ready to give me the answer when the guy on my left nudged me and said, "Excuse me, but—*do you mind?*"

I pulled my feet in, watching as he glided past my knees, down the stairs, and onto the stage where he stood beside Perseus. Beaming into the crowd as though he'd just ac-complished something majorly important and big, though I couldn't, for the life of me, even begin to guess what that might've possibly been.

And when the dorky guy in front of me made his way down too, I was surprised to see him greeted by a series of cheers and claps and even a couple wolf whistles along with a catcall or two. Then, just a moment after that, cheerleader girl turned to me, placed her hand right on my knee, and in her thick British accent said, "You're new 'ere, right?"

I nodded, even though I didn't really need to since she only paused for a second before she was talking again.

"I can always tell. But don't worry. Eventually *all* of yer questions will be answered. Every single one. But only *eventually*." She eyeballed me again, adding, "And not 'til yer ready." And before I could even respond, she was gone.

That radiant glow practically drifting behind her as she made her way down the stairs and onto the stage, smiling and waving at those of us still left sitting in the stands. Her gaze meeting mine and holding for a moment as she thought: *Just chill. The right person will find you and show you the way.* And then she turned toward dorky guy and whispered in his ear.

I gazed all around, wondering just exactly who that *right person* might be. Were they on the stage? In the stands? Or maybe even somewhere else entirely? And how did those people standing on the stage even know it was their turn to head down? I mean, it's not like I'd heard any summoning-type thoughts or any long list of names shouted out. Somehow, it just seemed as though everyone knew exactly where to go, when to go there, and what to do once they arrived.

Everyone seemed to know just exactly what was going on—and just exactly what it meant.

Everyone had a purpose.

Everyone but me.

To me, it all just seemed like a confusingly random, completely unrelated string of events.

But then, after watching a little bit longer, I realized that it might not be nearly as random as it first seemed, because everyone on that stage shared one thing in common.

One majorly big thing that the rest of us lacked.

They were all glowing.

Their bodies radiating the most beautiful, shimmering, deep green glow.

While the rest of us left sitting in the stands were made up of the varying shades of the ghostly pale spectrum.

I held my hands out before me and examined them closely just to make sure I wasn't missing something. But despite seeing a manicure desperately in need of a do-over, it was pretty much business as usual. Slim fingers, small knuckles, a freckle or two, but no glow in sight, not even a hint.

Once the stage was pretty much full, everyone around me stood in applause. And not wanting to appear totally clueless, I rose along with them. Jumping to my feet and covertly readjusting my blazer and smoothing my skirt, it wasn't long before it was over and I was merging along with the crowd once again, directing my question at anyone who might be kind enough to answer when I called out, "So—where to now?"

Hoping someone might be willing to pitch in and help out a newbie in need—give a little push in the right direction, or even the general direction would do—since I was beginning to feel even more clueless than when I first arrived at this place. And so far, nothing I'd seen resembled anything school-like, nor did it make the least bit of sense.

"We go to our assigned *place*, and you go to your assigned *place*," the guy before me said, glancing over his shoulder long enough to tack on a not-so-polite-sounding *"Where else?"* that immediately made my cheeks flush bright pink and my lips clamp tightly shut.

I took a deep breath (and no, I no longer had to breathe, but some habits really do die hard) and did my best to keep to myself and just shuffle along with the rest of them. My mind spinning with questions, wondering: Where the heck were we going—why was everyone acting so quiet and obedient—not to mention, just exactly where were these supposed friends my parents swore I'd find—the ones with common interests—the ones who liked to goof off and have a good time?

And the more I looked around, the more convinced I became that as far as schools went, this had to be the weirdest one of all.

And as far as the students went, well, they were weird too.

And there was just no getting around it—the whole thing was giving me a major case of the creeps.

I continued to gaze all around, desperate to find someone,

anyone, that I might be able to talk to, someone who might be able to clue me in to where we were all heading—and what I was in for once we got there.

But—nothing.

Most of them wouldn't even look at me, and the few who did merely smiled politely then quickly looked away. And it left me feeling so lonely and homesick, it felt like I had a vise shoved deep into my middle—one that was clamping down on my insides.

Still, I kept moving, placing one foot in front of the other, ignoring my worst fears, while trying to stay hopeful and bright (or at least appear that way), and to just allow myself to see where it led. But deep down inside, I was anxious, nervous, and more than a little scared, and all I really wanted was to head home, slip into my PJs, and curl up on my bed with Buttercup by my side.

The day I'd been dreading, the day my parents swore would open up a whole exciting new world, providing all of my favorite things, like art classes, and literature classes, and foreign language classes, and maybe even classes on singing, and acting, and dancing, and fashion design, and horseback riding too—the day that was supposed to make me forget all about my old life and happily embrace my new one—well, it was turning out just as I feared:

It was *awful*.

Nothing at all like they said it would be.

And it was pretty dang clear that when it came to these sorts of things, they really didn't have a clue. Nothing they'd promised could be found on the agenda—or at least not *my* agenda.

From everything I'd witnessed so far, this school was chock-full of bizarre rituals and bizarre glowing people who said bizarre things I couldn't even begin to comprehend. And any forced excitement that I may have started my day with, well, it was quickly snuffed out and completely obliterated by my absolute certainty that I didn't fit in.

Would never fit in.

And most certainly and positively, did *not* belong Here.

There had to be some other place better suited for me.

And not only was I sure of it, but I was determined to do whatever it took to find it.

5

After everyone disappeared, and I mean seriously, just took off in what seemed like a gazillion different directions, I decided to take cheerleader girl's advice and try to appear like a person who was just *chilling*. But the truth is, it was a total fake out. Because inside I felt all nervous and twitchy and more than a little humiliated to be standing there, all by myself, looking so lost and clueless like that.

Like a complete and total failure on my first day of school.

And I knew that anyone who saw me would agree it was true.

I plopped myself down on an elaborately carved wooden bench, acting as though I was just minding my own business as I took in the water-spouting, stone cherubs that lined the fountain before me, when what I was really doing was trying to decipher just what that cheerleader girl meant when she claimed the right person would find me and show me the way.

Did she mean like a guide?

Like a counselor or guardian angel of some kind?

And if so, was I supposed to do something to let them know I was Here? Ready, willing, and able to get this party started before I lost all my nerve and decided to head back home and never return?

The crowd thinned around me as I chewed on my nails in a way that instantly downgraded my manicure from ragged to downright pitiful. Not stopping until my nails were bitten to the quick, the quad was completely cleared, and it was just me and *him*—the dorky guy who had sat in front of me at the assembly.

The one who told me to *Shhh!*

The one with the greasy, slicked-back hair and black nerd frames perched high on his nose, the glass of which was so thick and heavy it obscured his eyes to the point where I could barely even see them.

The one with that deep, greenish glow who elicited a startling amount of catcalls and whistles as he made for the stage.

Though the longer I studied him, the more convinced I became that that little fan club of his was meant to be more ironic than real. And when I took in his dork shoes and weird, dark suit with the white shirt and skinny black tie that made

him look like he was either on his way to a nerd convention or a job interview with the CIA, I was sure.

And all I could think as he stood there before me was:

*Great! My first day of middle school, and I'm left with Monsieur Dorky Guy.*

And a *dead* dork at that.

Pretty much my biggest nightmare come true.

Temporarily forgetting the fact that thoughts are energy—that they can be heard by everyone Here until he turned to me and said, *"Dorky guy?"* Balking in a way that made his eyes bug out so much they practically pressed against his lenses, gaping at me as though he'd never been called that before, which, sorry to say, I found very hard to believe. "Did you seriously just call me a *dork*?" he repeated, clearly offended.

I stood there, lips screwed to the side, shoulders lifting in embarrassment, knowing there was no way to take it back, or at least not gracefully anyway. Deciding to just step up and own up when I said, "Well, maybe if you lost the suit and tie and ungreased your hair a little—you wouldn't look quite so—*er*—" I paused, reluctant to use the offending word yet again even though it was clearly the only one that would fit.

"*Dorkish? Dork-like?* Like the sole inhabitant of *Dorkville?*" He looked at me, brows merged, lips grim, and certainly not glowing like he did earlier. "Is that what you meant?"

I shrugged, unsure where to take it from there, but looking

right at him when I said, "Listen, I'm new, and this is all still a little confusing. Apparently I have some bad habits left over from the earth plane, and I haven't learned how to guard my thoughts yet, or even if that's actually possible. But the point is, I have no idea where I'm supposed to be, I just know I'm supposed to be somewhere. So, if you don't mind, I'm just gonna—"

I started to leave, started to push past him, but he just appeared right before me again in all of his four-eyed, greasy-haired *dorkitude*. Arms crossed tightly, head tilted to the side, as he slowly looked me over and said, "As it just so happens, I know exactly where you should be. You need to be following *me*."

I rolled my eyes, sincerely doubting that. Besides, no way was I following *him*. He was too weird, too dorky, and too obviously offended by the fact that I'd called him that. Standing my ground, I watched as he headed for this huge, all-glass pavilion. Taking the steep set of stairs in a handful of steps, just assuming I'd follow, which, eventually, left with no better options, I'm ashamed to admit, but I did.

"Hey—um—" I squinted at the back of his head, having no idea what to call him, but pretty sure that dorky guy was off-limits from this point on. "What is this place?" I asked, dreading the embarrassment of showing up late for my very first class where I'd instantly be pegged as the clueless new

girl for the rest of the year. "Seriously, where are you taking me?" I called, staring at his retreating back, seeing how he was pretty tall for his age, which I figured to be somewhere around fourteen even though he dressed more like somebody's dad.

Following him around a corner and stopping just short of bumping right into him when he paused before a large, smoked-glass door, opened it wide, and said, "They're all inside. Waiting for you."

I glanced between him and the door, seeing him nod encouragingly as I poked my head in and peered around at a big empty room where absolutely no one was waiting for me or anyone else for that matter. My eyes adjusting to the light as I took in the large, raised stage partially hidden by heavy, red velvet drapes, and the rows of soft, cushy chairs that faced it. And even though the room seemed perfectly nice, and not at all threatening in any way, shape, or form, I couldn't help but notice the awful feeling invading my middle, urging me to get the heck out of there, before it was too late.

And just as I turned to ask if this was some kind of hoax, some kind of lame pick-on-the-new-girl hazing ritual, he pressed his hand between my shoulder blades and shoved me inside.

Saying, "Good luck—you're gonna need it!" as the door slammed shut behind me.

# 6

I reached for the handle, eager to get the heck out so I could track him down and really let him have it. And I'd almost succeeded, when someone called out from behind me and I turned, scowl planted firmly in place, dreading even a moment's delay, only to find myself face-to-face with what I assumed to be an angel.

An incredibly beautiful, glittering angel.

The first one I'd seen since I'd arrived Here.

"Riley?" She looked at me with eyes so kind, I immediately eased the frown from my face. "You *are* Riley Bloom, right?"

I nodded. It was all I could do. I was so awed, so struck by her appearance, the way her long curly hair shimmered and shone, transforming from yellow to brown to black to red before starting the sequence all over again, while her skin did the same, converting from the palest white to the darkest ebony and everything else in between. And her gown, her beautiful, blue, sparkly gown, swished all around, gleaming in a way that made it look like it was woven from generous piles of stardust and long yards of lace. The only thing missing were wings, or if she had them, they weren't quite visible to me.

She smiled, beckoning for me to come closer, and I instantly followed without thinking twice. Because the truth is, she was so mesmerizing, so stunning, I just couldn't refuse. Radiating a light so brilliant, so vibrant, so deep, so—*purpley*—it made cheerleader girl and dorky guy seem like burned-out bulbs in comparison. And though I was sure I'd never met her before, she somehow seemed strangely familiar. And the moment she smiled, her kind eyes studying mine, I knew why—she was like every fairy-tale princess come to life.

"We're so very glad to see you," she said, hands folded before her.

*We?*

I blinked, once, twice, amazed to see the seats that had sat empty just a moment ago were now occupied by a small group of robe-clad people. But even though they glowed too, not one of them shined nearly as brightly as the beautiful angel before me.

"I'm Aurora," she said, and to be honest, I wasn't the least

bit surprised. If anyone could pull off a name like that, it was her. "And this here is Claude." She motioned toward a guy with a long, dark ponytail that pretty much matched the long, scraggly beard that hung almost to his waist. "And Royce." She nodded toward the guy next to Claude who, with his wavy brown hair, dark skin, and glinting green eyes, was definitely hot enough to be a major movie star back home on the earth plane. Samson was the guy sitting to his right, and honestly, he looked so old, he almost looked young again, like he'd come full circle or something, even though I know that doesn't really make any sense. And next to Samson was Celia, who was so petite, she seemed almost like a person in miniature, and her creamy silk robe was covered in the most beautiful embroidery of bright blossoming flowers and long, spindly vines.

But despite how kind, welcoming, and completely nonthreatening they all seemed, despite how they glowed in varying shades ranging from Celia's cornflower blue to Aurora's vibrant purple, I still couldn't ditch this increasingly uncomfortable feeling that lived inside me, though it's not like I could place it either. Nor could I come up with one good reason for having it in the first place. All I knew, as I stood there before them, was that something was up.

Something big.

And even though now, looking back, it all seems pretty obvious, at the time, I didn't have even the slightest clue of what I was in for.

From everything I'd seen up to that point, it didn't even occur to me that that kind of thing could actually be true.

"We're members of the Council," Aurora said, as though that somehow made sense, smiling as she took her seat among them. "Do you know what that is?"

I shook my head and bit down hard on my lip, unable to speak, unable to even *think* for that matter. Pretty much unable to do anything more than stand there and gape. My eyes darting around as I took in the room once again, gut practically going into spasms when I suddenly realized what the stage was for.

Why it just sat there all empty.

What this was *really* about.

"No worries," said the hot one, who I thought was named Royce but I was too freaked to be sure.

"Nothing to worry about. You're perfectly safe. None of us bite," said Samson, which, for some strange reason elicited a big laugh from everyone present.

Well, everyone except me.

I was about as far from laughing as a person could get. Because the truth is, I was too busy looking for a way out. Completely overcome by this horrible, sinking feeling, now that I had a pretty good idea of what my immediate future would bring.

And yet, that hard slab of fear in my gut was really no match for the rising wave of annoyance. The overwhelming feeling that I'd been Punk'd.

Sucker punched.

Set up in the most unfair way.

Remembering how just a little while earlier, my parents had simply hugged me good-bye as they sang *"have a nice day!"* as though everything were perfectly normal.

As though I wasn't about to be faced, *ambushed* really, with *this*.

No warning. No heads-up of any kind. Just tossed into a den of lions, with no ammo, no defenses, no tips on how to survive.

My gaze moved over them as I sighed and shook my head.

This was it.

Judgment day.

It was me against them and there was nothing I could do about it.

Not the least bit surprised when I suddenly found myself standing center stage even though I'd arrived there through no will of my own.

Watching in complete and total horror as they all leaned forward in their seats, eagerly waiting for the show to begin, as the drapes slid open behind me.

# 7

Claude, the bearded guy, got up from his seat, went over to the ginormous bookcase that lined the far wall that I somehow missed in my initial nervousness, and withdrew a small, slim book he casually flipped through. Proceeding to make a series of clicking sounds as his tongue hit the inside of his cheek, only to finally slam the book shut, place it back on the shelf, and return to his seat.

"Well, it seems someone's lived a *very* interesting life," he said, arranging his robe over his crossed legs as he looked at me. "Why don't you tell us a bit about that?"

I gaped, the eye-bugging, jaw-dropping kind of gape. Shooting him my best *you're crazy* look, sure that he had to be joking, even though the glint in his eyes assured me he was anything but.

They were waiting. All of them patiently waiting. Eager to

hear the extremely short story of my *over-before-I-knew-it* twelve years of life.

And the truth is, the longer they sat there, waiting for me to begin, the more annoyed I became, until the anger bubbled up so high inside me it boiled right over and spilled out when I said, "Are you *kidding me*?" I paused, waiting for someone to cop to it, to let me in on the joke, but when nobody did, I shook my head and continued. "How *interesting* could the story possibly *be* when I didn't even make it to *thirteen*?" I pressed my lips together to keep them from quivering in an embarrassing, visible way. Crossing my arms tightly across a chest that, now, thanks to the fact that I was sent Here, would stay stubbornly flat for, well, for eternity as far as I could tell. And when my eyes started to sting, and my throat went all hot and tight, it just made it all seem that much worse. I mean, the *one thing*—the *only* thing I ever really wanted was to be a teenager—and these people had yanked it right out from under me.

"So, is it accurate to say that you feel—*shortchanged*?" Royce asked, head cocked to the side, eyes all squinty. Studying me like he was the scientist and I his most interesting rat.

"Is that why you lingered so long on the earth plane?" asked Celia, in a polite, demure way, though I wasn't fooled for an instant. Not with the way her eyes roamed over me, not missing a thing.

And having them all staring at me like that, well, it just made it worse.

Made me feel like I was some kind of sideshow.

Some kind of freak.

Even though they were all striving to appear calm and thoughtful and friendly, as though they had all the time in the world for me to get my bearings and give them the big reveal of how I spent my twelve, pathetically short, years, I wasn't fooled for a second.

These people knew *everything*. It was all in the book. They just wanted to hear it from me. They wanted me to own up to it.

An afterlife test.

That's what this was.

There was no doubt in my mind.

"It's true that we know everything," Aurora confided, confirming what I'd already guessed. "But you have nothing to worry about, there's no judgment here. We just want to give you a chance to explain it, that's all. To tell us what motivated you to make the choices you did. We're interested in your input, to hear your side of things, so we can best decide where to *place* you."

I squinted, my gaze moving over them, *all* of them, but they were too good at this, too well practiced, and I couldn't glean even the slightest clue to what she might've meant by that.

"*Everyone* has a place," Celia said, her tiny hands smoothing the sleeves of her gown. "It is our task to find yours," she added, as though that should somehow mean something, as though that should make perfect sense to a newbie like me.

I shook my head, feeling completely annoyed, upset, and, well, mostly annoyed, saying, "Listen, I'm not really all that into this, so I'm wondering if we could maybe, um, catch up another time or something. I mean, since you already know all there is to know, I don't really see the point of all this. And, the truth is, I feel a little creeped out having to stand here on this stage. But fine, if you insist on knowing, then, okay, I guess the top two items on my short list of sins would probably be: *One,* sometimes, on certain occasions, I used to hog the mic when I played Rock Band on the Wii with my friends—" I stopped, hearing my own voice in my head saying, *Really? You're seriously going to lie about that? Here, of all places?* And clearing my throat when I added, "Um, okay, I might've actually hogged it more than *sometimes,* but that's only because I was practicing to go on *American Idol,* which, you probably don't know, but it's this really popular show on—" I shook my head, knowing I needed to keep it moving if I wanted to get out of there anytime soon.

"So, anyway, what else? Okay, well, I guess number two would be that one time, back in fourth grade, when we had that substitute teacher and someone, er, I mean *I,* changed the seating chart all around, so that all the girls had boy's names and all the boys had girl's names—but, again, I'd like to make it clear that there were extenuating circumstances in that case too. For starters, it wasn't entirely my idea. In fact, it wasn't my idea at all. But anyway, the only reason I even agreed to go along with it is because Felicia Hawkins dared me. And just in case you're unfamiliar with *her*, well, she is majorly mean. Seriously, she was one of the meanest, nastiest, snobbiest kids in the school, and, by the way, that includes all of the fifth and sixth graders too. So, with that in mind, I think it's fair to say that I really had no choice but to prove that I wasn't the least bit afraid of her, the substitute, or anyone else. Otherwise she would've been all over me for the rest of the year, if not longer. So, if anyone should be punished Here, it's Felicia Hawkins, *not me*. But *nooo*, she's still living, still breathing, and last I saw, still terrorizing her classmates, with no consequences whatsoever, while I'm the one who gets stuck Here, standing on some dumb stage, in some dumb room, defending a few dumb acts. I mean, seriously, how unfair is *that*?"

I stared at them, all flushed and red faced, but even though the question wasn't nearly as rhetorical as it may have seemed, not one of them answered. They just all leaned forward, practically in unison, like they'd rehearsed it or something, completely ignoring my overly emotional outburst that left me more than a little embarrassed, as their eyes focused on the screen just behind me. A screen that suddenly flickered to life, showing a stream of images of—

Well—

*Me.*

*Me,* at home in Eugene, Oregon, not even a year old and crawling after my big sister Ever who was just four years older and from what I could see, already mourning the loss of her privacy.

*Me,* a few years later, pedaling furiously on my new purple bike with the training wheels attached, doing my best to keep up with Ever, whose bike was lime green and a heck of a lot faster than mine.

*Me,* a few years later still, sneaking Ever's clothes and wearing them to school without her knowing, even though they didn't exactly fit and I had to roll up the hems and the sleeves.

*Me,* just last year, not long before the accident, spying on her and her old boyfriend Brandon with a mixture of fascination and revulsion as they kissed on the couch in our den when our parents were having one of their "date nights" and she was supposed to be babysitting me.

And honestly, I have no idea what the Council might've been thinking, but as for *me,* I was mortified. Unable to tear my eyes away from the screen of horrors that unfolded before

me, and cringing with embarrassment as I watched an un-mistakable pattern of behavior I'd never realized before.

A pattern of behavior I actually swore, time and again, didn't actually exist.

Having successfully convinced myself it was Ever who wouldn't stop bugging me, who practically lived just to tor-ment me, and wouldn't leave me alone no matter how much I complained.

But at that moment, watching the no-holds-barred, well-documented truth play out before me—well, there was no denying the fact that I'd spent the majority of my ridiculously short life stalking her, spying on her, copying her, and pretty much bugging her to the point of harassment.

Over a decade spent in one, long, pitiful attempt to be just like her.

My insides churned as fresh new images filled up the screen, each one that streamed past as equally humiliating as the one just before it. Causing me to wrap my arms around my waist, wanting to make myself smaller, to disappear, to be anywhere but there in that room, on that stage. Feeling all nauseous and clammy, like that time I got seasick at the lake.

My whole life had been a lie.

Not at all what I'd thought.

And there was just no hiding from that fact anymore.

Sure there were other moments mixed in, ones where

43

Ever was off somewhere with her friends while I hung out with mine. But, for the most part, well, it was completely unbalanced, and there was just no getting around it.

As far as little sisters went, I was your everyday, garden-variety, textbook, pain in the bum.

"Are these like—edited—or maybe even, um, you know, Photoshopped, or something?" I asked, my voice going all high and screechy, in what my mom used to call my *liar's voice*. The one I used when the last cookie was gone and I was under suspicion, or the house was a mess and I'd been the only one home. And don't think the members of the Council didn't notice.

I hung my head low and turned away from the screen, knowing there was nothing more to do. Nothing more to say. It was all over now, and all I could do was sit back and wait to learn just what would become of me.

8

It wasn't over.

It seemed like it should've been.

I wanted it to be.

But *noooo*. Not even close.

Just as I was awaiting the verdict to come down, this scratchy, staticky kind of sound came at me from all four walls, and I couldn't help it, no matter how much I didn't want to see it, I looked. Peering over my shoulder, and seeing the way the images suddenly changed, going all hazy and misty as the light dimmed to a yellowy glow I immediately recognized. My insides curling in on itself like a fist, instinctively knowing that no matter how bad it had seemed just a few moments before, things had just taken a major turn for the worse.

They'd caught me in Summerland too.

That mystical dimension between the earth plane and this

one where I lingered for—well, let's just say I stayed there for much longer than I was supposed to.

And so I watched.

Watched what they watched.

*Me,* newly dead, but still up to my old tricks as though my early departure hadn't made the slightest bit of difference. Hadn't hampered me in any way.

Hadn't changed a single thing.

If anything, being dead had just made me even *worse.* Granting me the kind of access I could've only dreamed of before.

It was like having a backstage pass to not only my sister's life, but everyone else's as well. Spying on old neighbors and friends, former classmates, favorite and not-so-favorite teachers, even a few well-known celebrities—just maximizing my invisibility for all it was worth. And just like before, back when I was alive, I'd spent the bulk of my time spying on my sister, completely unaware that I was being spied on as well.

My entire existence, my birth, my death, and beyond, had been documented and studied, and now I was expected to find a way to explain (if not justify), what clearly amounted to a heckuva lot of wasted time.

But the truth is, I had no idea what to say for myself.

I was the most surprised person in that whole entire room.

And, when we got to the part where I sneaked into the

Viewing Room on my way to school—well, I just sank right down there onto the cold, hard stage, not even bothering to manifest a comfortable chair for myself first. Anxiously waiting for this horrible show to finally end, so that they could determine my *place*.

The whole room went silent as the screen went blank, and I knew it was up to me to make the first move.

"Well, I think the footage speaks for itself, no?" I tried to smile, but it felt all sloppy and wrong. So then I tried to give them my big-eyed, sad look, the one that always worked on my dad—but still, nothing. They just sat there, so silent and still it was clear I'd have to do much better than that.

I wouldn't be let off so easily.

So I cleared my throat and focused hard on my shoes, saying, "Okay, so maybe I was a bit of a brat." I shrugged, trying to keep it casual and relaxed. "But the thing is, last time I checked that wasn't exactly listed as one of the sins, right?" I looked up, desperate for a little confirmation, understanding, *something*, and I found it in Aurora—the one person I could count on, the one I chose to focus on. "I mean, maybe if you guys had allowed me just a few more years, I could've turned it around. Maybe I would've even done something great, something truly tremendous and world changing, you know? But now—well, now, we'll never know just what I was capable of, since, you know, you called me out so early in the game." I sighed, partly for dramatic effect, and partly because, well, the whole thing was a little exhausting. And when that was also met with more stares and silence I said, "Okay, fine. You want to know the truth? Well, here it is. I feel like I was robbed! Seriously. Dead at twelve? That is so *not* fair! And why am I the one who's expected to explain *my* actions anyway? I was just a kid—I was supposed to be immature! But you guys—well, maybe one of you should explain a few things to me. Maybe I'm the one who deserves some answers Here? Huh? Did anyone ever stop and think of *that*?" I stopped, panting and agitated, and it's not like I needed a mirror to know that my face was beet red.

I concentrated on my shoes again, shaking my head as I pledged a strict vow of silence from that point on. Pledging that no matter what happened next, I wouldn't say another word—wouldn't try to defend a single thing that I'd done. My life as I knew it was over, and there was no taking it back. No do-overs allowed. Which meant there was really no point to any of this. It was tortuous, and mean, and completely unfair, and no way was I giving them any more ammo to use against me than they already had.

I continued to sit there, firmly committed to maintaining my silence and waiting it out for as long as it took, when Aurora finally looked at me and said, "I know you may not understand it just yet, but in time you will. It'll all make perfect sense, I promise you that. But for now, just know that everything works out in the way it's supposed to. There is no punishment, no harsh judgment, and no accidents of any kind. All is as it should be. We're just trying to understand things from your point of view, to study your life with compassion, not discrimination. All of us realize just how hard it is to find one's way in the earth plane—there are so many distractions, so many directions in which to turn. We don't condemn a single one of your acts, Riley, so there's no reason to be fearful or angry. We're merely attempting to understand you better, that's all."

My gaze met hers, and yes she was kind, and nice, and oh so glowy and angelic, but I needed something more. I refused to be brushed off so easily.

"And so, it's my destiny to be *dead*?" I said, immediately breaking my vow of silence and wondering if my tendency toward *mouthiness*, as my mom calls it, would get me in as much trouble Here as it did there.

But Aurora just smiled as the rest of the group took a moment to chuckle among themselves, which, truth be told, did *not* make me feel even the slightest bit better since it's not like I was trying to be funny.

"It'll all make sense in due time," Claude with the long, scraggly beard piped in, propping his bare feet on the seat just before him as he added, "but for now, do you have anything to say on your behalf? Any comments about what you just saw up on the screen?"

My shoulders drooped. *All* of me drooped. I was done with words and out of excuses. I just wanted it to end. To learn my *place*, and move on.

They gazed at each other, communicating in a way that was completely blocked from me, finally coming to some sort of mutual agreement when they nodded toward Celia, who turned to me and said, "Based on your accumulated history and your strong attachment to the earth plane, you will train as a Catcher. Any questions?"

*Train as a—what?* A question that was soon followed by a gazillion others just like it.

"A *Soul* Catcher," Samson said, pushing his long silver hair off his face and settling his violet eyes right on mine. Adding, "A catcher of souls." As if that made any more sense.

And I was just about to ask the obvious, when Aurora cut in with her soft, soothing voice that made every word sound like the most perfectly chosen lyric to a beautiful song, and said, "Riley, your situation is not as unique as you think. There are plenty of souls who resist the call to come Here. Many of whom are still wandering the earth plane, unwilling to cross the bridge and move on. Some resist for centuries, ignoring any and all attempts to lure them Here, while some only linger for a short time. And while each individual soul is granted free will, every now and then we find they require a little extra . . . *push*, if you will. A little reminder that they have choices, better choices, than those that they've chosen. And that's where you come in."

My eyes darted between them, and even though I was brimming with questions, lots and lots of questions, it's like I had so many I had no idea where to begin. All I knew for sure is that I was going *back*.

Back to the earth plane.

The *glorious* earth plane!

And as far as I was concerned, I couldn't leave soon enough.

"We've no doubt that carefully guided and given the proper training, you'll be a very successful Soul Catcher for us," Royce said, granting me a smile that was made for spotlights, movie screens, and magazine covers as the others nodded their agreement.

"So, when do I leave?" I jumped to my feet, suddenly brimming with an abundance of energy that was lacking just a few moments earlier. "When do I get my old life back?" I asked, picturing myself moving right back into the old neighborhood and enrolling in my old school, not quite sure how all the logistics would work. You know, how they would go about fixing the fact of my being dead one day, and, well, pretty much *undead* the next. Then dismissing it just as quickly, figuring that to be their problem, not mine.

Me, I was fulfilling a mission.

A *very* exciting mission.

But my excitement barely had a chance to take hold when Aurora looked at me, her brown/red/black/silver/blond hair swirling around her in a whirl of waves and rivulets as she said, "You will return in spirit form only. Invisible to all but your fellow spirits, and the gifted few who are able to sense us."

My eyelids grew heavy, my shoulders sank, and I sighed. Deflated, disappointed, disillusioned—not one of those words even begins to describe how I felt. And yet, I was still going back. There was no changing that. If the Council saw fit to send me packing, well, who was I to fight it, no matter what form I'd be in?

And from what I'd seen so far of this school, with the assembly and the singing and the glowing, and all the other accumulated weirdness, well, I figured I wouldn't really miss it.

"When do I leave?" I asked, instantly ashamed when I realized I hadn't given a second thought to what I would tell my parents and grandparents until the words were already out.

"No reason to delay," Celia said, checking with the others who nodded their agreement.

"The sooner the better," Samson chimed in.

"Now would be good," agreed Royce.

And even though I was excited, I still had to ask, "But, what about my family? What'll I tell them?"

Turning as Claude motioned toward the screen that was now split down the middle—one side showing my dad enjoying some kind of jam session with a bunch of other musicians, while the other side showed my mom painting in some brightly lit studio, her smock splattered with virtually every color in the rainbow as a smile lit up her face. And even though I had no idea what it meant, my insides started to do that weird clenching/curling thing again.

I pressed my lips together, trying to make sense of what I was seeing. Wondering why they weren't where they said they would be, why they'd choose to lie and play hooky from what they'd told me. But then, before I could blink, the screen split again, and I saw each set of grandparents engaged in some pretty surprising activities of their own, especially once their age was factored in. Enjoying stuff like: surfing, and hiking, and ranching, and symphony composing, as well as overseeing a nursery full of brand-spanking newborns.

"They've already been *placed*," Aurora said. "They're enjoying their *soul* work now. There's no need to worry about them."

*Soul work?* I blinked. Things were getting weirder by the second. I mean, initially, I was worried about them worrying about me. But from what I could see, I'd be surprised if they even noticed I was gone.

"Your family already understands what's just now becoming clear to you. Sometimes, back on the earth plane, real life gets in the way of who we are truly meant to be, but Here you can do what you've always dreamed of, you can fulfill your destiny." She smiled.

And even though she clearly thought this was a Really Great Thing, and clearly expected for me to agree—I didn't.

I couldn't.

Knowing all of that just made me feel even more alone, completely unnecessary, and more than a little *unwanted*.

"So—you're saying that back home, back on the earth plane, me, and Ever, and Buttercup—*got in the way?*" Instantly ashamed by the way my voice suddenly cracked, but still, the whole idea of it made my insides go all weird again.

But Aurora just smiled, as did everyone else, nodding toward Celia who said, "Of course not."

"Your parents and grandparents love you, and they wouldn't change a thing!" Samson nodded.

"But Here, you have your own guide, which frees your family up to live out their destinies. It doesn't all end with death, you know. We have tasks, things to accomplish, learning to do. Your parents have found their *place*, and now

you've found yours. All is as it should be," Royce said, pressing his hands together and bowing toward me.

"But—what about my *house*? And—and my *dog*—" I shook my head, unable to finish, unable to understand how it got to this point. At first I was so excited, sure I'd won the afterlife lottery by getting to go back, only to have it all ripped out from under me as everything familiar slipped away too.

"You're free to come back and visit between assignments," Aurora said, glowing in the most beautiful, mesmerizing way. "And Buttercup," she smiled, "is free to travel alongside you."

"Really?" I cocked my head to the side, wondering how Buttercup might feel about that. "Does he have a destiny to fulfill too?" I asked.

Only to be met by the sound of Royce's deep, hearty laugh when he shook his head and said, "Dogs are a gift to mankind. They are happy and joyful and loyal by nature. They are pure, positive energy and teach by example. That is all that's required of them."

I nodded, doing my best to take it all in. It may not have been what I'd first thought, or even what I'd hoped for, but still, it could've been a lot worse.

My thoughts interrupted by Aurora when she said, "Riley, how about we let go of your past and look instead toward your future. What do you say? Are you ready to make that leap?"

And before I could answer, before I could do much of anything, Buttercup ran out from behind the red velvet curtain, tail wagging like mad, licking my face, and knocking me down in the way that always made me laugh. And by the time I finally got him to calm down, everyone was gone.

Not even waiting long enough for me to respond.

And that's when I realized the question had been rhetorical.

My place had been determined.

Whether I liked it or not.

# 9

I stood outside with Buttercup beside me, both of us on high alert, waiting for some kind of sign.

Both of us equally clueless with absolutely no idea where to go, which way to turn, or what to do next.

And while it may seem weird for a person to look to their dog for guidance, the thing was, Buttercup's the one that led my family to the bridge. He's the one that leaped across first. So, with that in mind, I figured he might have some kind of unique, canine ability, some kind of yellow Lab instinct. Like a dog-only radar for these kinds of things.

But nope, he just sat there with his big brown eyes and pink nose, blinking at me as I gazed all around, thinking how a little instruction, a little *guidance* of some sort would've been nice.

But *nooo*.

The Council just vanished, just completely disappeared.

Who even knew where they went?

All I knew was that between me and Buttercup we hadn't a clue how we were supposed to get from Here to There.

Was I supposed to just *wish* it—just *desire* it like everything else in this place? Or was there some kind of regularly scheduled transportation, like a bus, or a train, or even some kind of wings we could rent?

All I knew for sure was that the bridge I had crossed over to make the trip Here was strictly a one-way-only kind of thing. And I know this because I happened to look back the second I'd made it to the other side.

I wasn't nearly as committed to the crossing as I'd pretended to be.

Only it was too late.

It'd completely vanished from sight.

Never to be seen again.

So, with no signs headed our way, I made for the nearest building instead. Motioning for Buttercup to follow along, figuring we should try to look for someone who might be willing to help, and we were just about halfway there when I heard:

"So, how'd it go? Did you cry? Grovel? Promise you could do better if only they'd give you another chance?"

My gaze narrowed, as my lips pressed tightly together, watching as dorky guy came up from behind me, head bent,

clump of greasy hair swooping into his face as he paused to clean his glasses with the end of his tie. And I hate to admit it, but for that split second, he actually looked really different, almost like someone you'd call, well, *cute.*

But like I said, it didn't last. It was pretty much over in a flash, and a moment later, the glasses were in place, his hair was greased back, and he returned to being dorky guy again.

"Why do you even wear those, anyway?" I motioned toward his thick, nerd frames, purposely ignoring his question. I had no intention of confiding anything about my life review to him, or anything else for that matter. In fact, I couldn't wait to get myself to the earth plane where I'd never have to see him again. I was really looking forward to that. "Can't you just *wish* for better eyesight? Or maybe try to *manifest* a cooler pair of glasses?" I looked at him, waiting for a response, but when he failed to answer, I said, "Seriously, there are much cooler frames you could wear, fashions have really advanced in the last several—*decades*—you'd be amazed!" I nodded, assuring myself I was veering much closer to helpful than judgmental. Just stating the facts as I so clearly saw them. "I mean, it's pretty obvious you haven't been anywhere near the earth plane, since—" I scrunched my brow and squinted, he was so out of date I couldn't even guess when he was last seen alive.

"What happened to you anyway?" I asked. "How'd you

end up here? Did you go head to head with a newly sharpened number two pencil? Did you accidentally choke yourself with your tie? Or, perhaps you actually *died* of the embarrassment of wearing clothes like that?" I shook my head and laughed, I couldn't help it—sometimes I really crack myself up. And even though he failed to join in, that didn't stop me from saying, "You do know you can manifest a whole new wardrobe, right? We're really not bound to the mistakes of our past. So go ahead, knock yourself out. Just close your eyes and ask—*What would Joe Jonas wear?*"

But even though that last part really got me going, like the bent-over, thigh-slapping kind of going, my laughter was soon halted by the sound of him saying, "If you have to know, it was cancer. The big bad C did me in. Osteosarcoma—or bone cancer, as most people know it. They even removed my leg in an attempt to save me, but it was too late, it'd already spread all over the place."

I gulped, my eyes locked on his, knowing I should say something, anything, but no words would come. Telling myself he was just one of many. That this place was full of sad stories like his. Every tragic ending found its way Here. But still, it didn't make me feel the slightest bit better. I'd had no right making fun of him like I did.

"I was well on my way to going pro too." He shrugged. "It was back in 1999—missed the millennium, the timing

couldn't have been worse." He looked at me and shook his head, his gaze so matter-of-fact, bearing not the slightest trace of ill will or regret. "But that's how it goes sometimes, right?"

I nodded, weakly, I didn't know what else to do. And even though I was curious as to just what kind of *pro* he was talking about, I was far too uncomfortable to ask.

I just stood there, watching as he turned, glanced at Buttercup sitting patiently beside me, and said, "Seriously? You're bringing the dog?'

I rolled my eyes, my mood going from shamed to annoyed in a fraction of a second, as I looked all around, wondering where the hall monitors were. At my old school, you'd never get away with this kind of harassment, this kind of covert bullying and truancy. But Here, it seemed like pretty much anything goes. Like we were all on some kind of honor system or something.

Motioning for Buttercup to follow along as I turned and called out behind me, "For your information, the *dog* has a name—it's *Buttercup*." I glared, shooting him my best over-the-shoulder death stare. "As for the rest, well, it's really none of your business now is it?"

I picked up the pace, eager to put some distance between us, but it didn't make the slightest bit of difference. No matter how fast I went, he was right there beside me, looking at me when he said, "Well, I can see why you might think that, but you're wrong. It *is* my business. All potential travelers must be cleared by me. I decide who gets in and who doesn't. Think of me as the bouncer for this particular trip."

"Dressed like that, it's pretty much impossible to think of you as anything other than dorky guy," I mumbled, taking a moment to roll my eyes at Buttercup, completely annoyed by his tendency to be overly affectionate toward strangers, especially *this* stranger. Going so far as to actually sniff, then lick dorky guy's hand, carrying on like the worst kind of traitor.

"And another thing, this whole dorky guy thing? It ends *now*. I have a name, and I'd like for you to use it," he said, appearing right before me again.

I stopped, there was no use running a race I couldn't win. Hands clutching my plaid-covered hips when I said, "Yeah? So, let's hear it. What would you like me to call you instead?"

"Bodhi." He nodded, seemingly pleased with the sound of it.

"Bodhi," I repeated, thinking that as far as names went, it was a good one. Only thing is, it didn't work. In fact, everything about it was wrong. Bodhi conjured up images of cute, tan, surfer boys, like the ones who live in Ever's Laguna Beach neighborhood. The kind who were pretty much the opposite of Mr. Pocket Protector with the bad hair, worse glasses, and nerdy clothes who stood right before me.

"Seriously," he said, eyes narrowed on mine for a moment

before he looked around nervously. "You *have* to stop this. I heard every word of that—and so did—" He paused, gritting his teeth to keep from saying anything more. His gaze locked on mine when he added, "Listen, all you need to know is that *I'm* your guide. I'm the one you've been looking for. Think of me as your teacher, guidance counselor, coach, and boss, all rolled into one. Which means you *cannot* continue to talk to me like that, or to call me that. There will be consequences for that sort of insubordination. Serious consequences. So just stop—okay? My name is Bodhi, and I expect you to use it. You need to—" He hesitated, his eyes darting all around in the most paranoid way, his voice lowered to a whisper when he said, "You need to *respect* me, okay?"

I squinted, alerted to the undercurrent of begging that rang loud and clear, with just a pinch of paranoia thrown in for good measure.

*So this is my guide,* I thought, sucking in a mouthful of air, wondering what other punishments might be in store. I mean, he had no wings, no shimmering robe, no halo, nothing that indicated he should in any way be the boss of me, and yet, there it was. He *was* the boss of me. And despite my wanting to believe otherwise, somehow I just knew it was real. Somehow I just knew he wasn't lying about this.

"So, you're like my guardian angel then? For real?" I watched as he shrugged, obviously uninterested in the details.

And something about him, something about the slouchy way he stood—not bad-posture slouchy—not low-self-esteem slouchy—but more like cool guy with a cool name slouchy—just didn't fit with his overall look.

Something was weird about him.

*Off.*

Something I couldn't quite put my finger on.

"Listen," he said, eager to move on. "It's my job to teach you everything, if you want to get to the next level, that is. And believe me, you have *a lot* to learn before you can even think about that. But, first things first—we need to get moving. Are you ready to head back to the earth plane?" He buried his hands in his pockets and looked all around, obviously as eager to *vámanos* out of this place as I was.

"The next *level*?" I eyeballed him carefully, as I walked alongside him. "What's that supposed to mean?"

But he was already ten steps ahead. Glancing over his shoulder to say, "All in good time, Riley. All in good time."

# 10

It took a trolley, a tram, a bus, and a subway just to get part of the way there.

Or at least I called it the subway.

Bodhi called it the tube.

While the guy who checked our tickets called it the tunnel.

So who really knew?

All I knew for sure is that I was more than a little disappointed there wasn't any flying involved.

And I don't mean flying on an airplane flying, I mean the kind of flying usually reserved for birds, or butterflies, or angels, or maybe even dead people like me.

The kind of flying you sometimes get to experience in your dreams, when you just take off and start soaring through the clouds for no apparent reason.

That's the kind of flying I was hoping for.

And when it didn't happen, when I realized we'd be stuck

with the same old methods of transportation I'd known back home, well, I'm not even sure why I was so disappointed. Especially since, up to that point anyway, nothing in the afterlife was anything at all like I'd expected. So why would flying be any different?

"Wrong again," Bodhi said, eavesdropping on my thoughts, which, by the way, was really starting to get on my nerves in a very big way. I mean, it was bad enough knowing my entire existence had been documented, but having what I once thought of as my private thoughts so easily accessed by my afterlife guide, well, it really bugged me.

"There *is* flying." He nodded, not bothering to push his hair back when it fell into his face yet again, just leaving it to hang there, dangling before his glasses, like a thick, greasy noodle. "And trust me, it's as fun as you think, if not funner."

"*Funner?*" My eyes grew wide as a smile pulled at my lips. "You sure about that—that it's actually *funner?*"

I couldn't help it, I just burst out laughing right there in front of him. And I'm talking the eye-squinching, belly-clutching kind of laughing. But he just ignored me, and continued yammering on and on as though I hadn't even called him out on his grammar.

"It doesn't require wings like you think," he said, straightening his legs until they took up the two empty seats on the aisle right across from me and dangled off the end.

"So, when do *I* get to fly?" I asked, calming myself down enough to look right at him.

Watching as he leaned down to scratch Buttercup between the ears, glancing at me when he said, "All in good time."

I rolled my eyes, already sick of the phrase and correctly assuming I hadn't even come close to hearing the last of it. Scrunching way down in my seat, bringing my knees to my chest, and wrapping my arms tightly around them as I stared out the window, trying to grasp hold of the passing scenery, to pause it, to make sense of it, but the train was moving so fast it was hard to grasp any one thing in particular. Still, I had this sort of inner sense of a whole stream of images. Like a continuous flow of pictures, events that happened on the earth plane, including stuff that was both way before me, and way after me.

The entire story of mankind.

The history of time.

And even though it was impossible to tell just how long the journey took, it didn't seem like it took all that long. Or at least not nearly as long as you'd think a trip like that would take. And before I knew it we were out of the tunnel, off of the tube, and standing on a platform as Bodhi looked all around us and said, "This is it."

A gush of wind swept past me as the train we'd just disembarked vanished from sight, leaving the three of us gazing all around, trying to get our bearings in a place that, while I was sure it was part of the earth plane, didn't look even the slightest bit familiar.

I stayed focused on Bodhi, hoping he knew where he was going as he wordlessly led us down one street, and then another, before reaching a long, narrow alleyway which eventually let out onto a narrow cobblestone lane. He pointed up toward the sky and said, "That's it." Then he paused for a moment before adding, "I think."

"You—*think*?" I narrowed my eyes, the miniscule amount of confidence I'd granted him gone, just like *that*.

"No, I'm sure of it. Really. That's *definitely* it," he repeated, straightening his shoulders and nodding firmly, trying to appear certain, commanding, like a confident sure-footed guide, but still I had the sinking feeling he was as clueless as Buttercup and I.

"So, what is *it* exactly?" I said, following past the tip of his pointing finger, trying to squint through the clouds, gray skies, and extreme fog but not getting very far.

"That, right up there." He continued to point into the distance, at what I was sure was nothing in particular. "That's where we need to be. Warmington Castle. That's where he lives."

"*He?*" I turned, taking him in, fully aware of Buttercup pressing himself hard against my legs in a way that told me he didn't feel any better about this than I did.

Watching as Bodhi smiled, closed his eyes, and manifested two skateboards, a black one for him, and a purple one for me. Wasting no time before jumping onto his and glancing over his shoulder as he said, "Your first subject awaits. The Radiant Boy. Now follow me, and try to keep up."

11

All I can say about the skateboarding is that Bodhi did not ride *at all* like I'd assumed he would. Because to be honest, I expected to see a pretty bad spectacle—a real wince-worthy display. But the truth is, he didn't fall, didn't wipe out, didn't even falter the slightest bit.

On the contrary, he did so many loops and turns and spins and tricks—it was all I could do to keep pace.

I guess I just didn't see that coming.

I was stunned in every conceivable way.

And just in case you think it can all be attributed to the fact that he's dead—well, think again. I'm dead too, and I could barely stay upright, much less loop and spin my way up and down those winding, swooping, curving hills. Nope, that was pure skill on his part, a skill I clearly lacked. And by the time we'd reached the top, I watched as he clicked the end of his board in a way that made it flip effortlessly into his hand as he looked me over and said, "Told you I was about to go pro." He tilted his head, motioning toward the building before us. "So, what do you think? It's pretty amazing, isn't it?"

I nodded. Because even though it was my first castle, a fact that left me pretty much in awe and eager to be impressed, it was obviously one of the good ones. Made of smooth, grayish stone, it was tall and impressive and seemed like it meandered forever. Dotted with lots and lots of those high, pointy towers I think they call turrets. The only thing missing was a moat filled with alligators, but I was willing to overlook that.

I swallowed hard, unsure if I really was ready for this. I mean, if I lived in a place this amazing, I might not be so willing to give it up either.

Keeping a nervous eye on Buttercup who was off sniffing and marking the extensive, well-manicured grounds, I cleared my throat and said, "So, what exactly is it we're doing here anyway?" Discreetly kicking my skateboard under a nearby bush, hoping I wouldn't be required to use it again anytime soon.

"This is where he lives," Bodhi said, his voice filled with reverence. "The Radiant Boy. He's been here for years. Centuries, really."

"Why do you call him that?" I squinted, more interested in delaying than in getting the actual answer.

"Because that's his name." He shrugged, chewing on his bottom lip in this weird way that he has.

"So, you're telling me that his mom actually named him the *Radiant Boy*?" I shook my head and rolled my eyes, fingers drumming against my wool, plaid skirt. "No wonder he's still here, still haunting the place. He's angry. He wants a do-over. A second chance with a better name. It's not his fault. The kid got a bum deal."

Bodhi peered at me from the corner of his eye, clearly not amused. "No one knows his real name, or even where he came from. All that's known about him is that he's spent hundreds of years scaring people. The how and why is a mystery, and that's where you come in."

He turned toward me, staring right into my bugged-out eyes and wide-open mouth. My guide, my boss, my teacher, my coach, whatever he was, whatever authority he claimed to have over me, I sincerely doubted he truly had the power to just expand upon my job description like that. The Council already told me I'd be trained as a Soul Catcher, one who catches earthbound souls and makes them move on. That's it. No one ever said anything about learning people's personal histories, motivations, or solving mysteries of any kind.

"Last I heard, it was my duty to lead him to the bridge, nothing more, nothing less," I said, wanting him to know, before this went any further, that while he may shame me when it came to skateboarding, I was not one to be messed with.

He smiled. Well, he *almost* smiled—his lip lifting just the tiniest bit at each corner, before dropping back down again. "And, just how exactly do you plan to do that without gaining his trust first?" he asked.

I gulped. I hadn't really thought about that. Hadn't really thought about much of anything past returning to the earth plane again. And now that I'd made it, and realized the enormity of my task, well, let's just say it was making me start to miss my new school, Perseus, cheerleader girl, tunic boy, and all that went with it.

I swallowed hard, suddenly feeling very small and inadequate, unsure if I was really equipped to handle any of this.

And it's not like Bodhi was about to make it easier. He just went on and on, like some narrator in one of those boring documentary films they make you watch on rain days at school, saying, "He's known to be a golden-haired specter who actually glows in the dark, and the legends all claim that seeing him is an omen of misfortune or doom. Though, in the last century, that seems to be disproven, as many people have seen him and not one of them, or at least not yet anyway, have, um, found their doom—so to speak. Also, there are more rumors about him maybe being German and perhaps

even murdered by his own mother, but again, that's just purely speculation. What I can tell you for sure is that there've been many accounts of a series of Radiant Boys haunting various castles in both Cumberland and Northumberland counties, but my guess is that all those others are fakes, a lie started by the castle owners in an attempt to compete with Warmington and try to draw business and put themselves on the map. Not to mention how—"

"Wait—what counties did you say?" I asked, gazing at the large stone castle before me, and stalling in the very worst way.

"Some counties here in England. Anyway, they also say—"

"Wait—we're in *England*?" I looked at him, eyes wide with excitement. That was the first good news I'd heard all day. Bodhi nodded, eager to continue with his lecture, but I wasn't interested. I was still stuck on the part that I'd just made my first international trip. "So, can we check out London? After we're done with—um, pushing the Radiant Boy across the bridge?" I asked, discreetly crossing my fingers and hoping we could, because that would make it all worthwhile. That would be really, really cool.

Bodhi frowned, clearly annoyed, saying, "Yeah, sure, whatever. But first you need to pay attention. You need to know just what you're dealing with here. Not to mention how nobody is *pushing* anybody anywhere. You will *coax* him, and *convince* him; he has to cross over on his own volition."

I glanced at Bodhi, thinking how funny it was how one minute he was like any other normal fourteen-year-old kid using words like *funner*, and the next he was all serious and businesslike, using words like *volition*. And as someone who also likes to mix up my vocabulary a bit, I decided I'd like him for that.

But only for that.

I gazed up at the castle, overcome by excitement.

I was going to London!

Home of Robert Pattinson, Daniel Radcliffe, Princes William and Harry, not to mention my dad's all-time favorite band, the Beatles (okay, maybe, technically, they were from Liverpool—but still, it was close enough for me).

All I had to do was rid this place of a ghost and I was *there*. Convince some pampered mama's boy with an unfortunate name who refuses to give up the big house with the fancy gardens and fountains and pointy-topped turrets to move on to, well, from what I'd seen of it, a really weird school and a really uncomfortable life review.

And in that moment, I *knew* I could do it. Easy peasy. I had all the motivation I'd need. I mean, seriously, I was so suddenly sure of myself, I was just brimming, overflowing with confidence.

Cutting off Bodhi's never-ending speech when I said, "Okay, so let's cut to the chase here. What exactly am I

dealing with? Just how old is this kid?" Figuring it was best to go in with a plan, and knowing his age would tell me just how to approach him.

Either he was younger than me, and therefore less scary, maybe even completely inferior in every way. Or he was older, and, well, I'd have a little more work cut out, but nothing I couldn't handle for sure.

"I don't know." Bodhi sighed. "Nobody knows. This kid's a real enigma, a complete and total mystery. But some say he appears to be around ten."

"*Ten?*" I gaped, glancing between the castle and Bodhi. I could hardly believe my good luck. This kid, this scary *ghost* kid, was only *ten*? "Please." I laughed, shaking my head and allowing for a slow, dramatic roll of my eyes. "I remember *ten.*" I blew my bangs off my face, squared my shoulders, and straightened my skirt, preparing myself to go in. "So, where is he? Where's this *scary* little ten-year-old kid? Let me at him. I've got a trip to London waiting for me."

Bodhi looked at me, obviously weighing something in his mind. Clearly deciding against whatever it was, when he shrugged and said, "Fine, we'll do it your way. For now. Follow me."

## 12

Buttercup and I followed him across a large garden, cutting across a path of carefully trimmed hedges that made for a pretty complicated maze for those who couldn't just walk straight through them like we could. Continuing right past the thick stone wall and emerging on the other side into a huge, oversized room with a super high ceiling, large stained-glass windows, threadworn rugs, dusty chandeliers, and, like, a ton of old things that I guessed to be priceless antiques.

"He's said to haunt the blue room," Bodhi whispered, even though no one was present and no one could hear us. His eyes darting all around until he spied the large, sprawling staircase, dropped his board, and skated toward it.

"So, this place has so many rooms they have to color code them?" I asked, having visited more than a few celebrity mansions in my earlier dead days, but never an actual castle, never anything quite so big and sprawling and amazing as this.

But Bodhi just shrugged, having already reached the top of the landing and tilting his head to the right as he said, "If I remember correctly, it's that way, third door on the left."

I stopped. Stopped right there in my tracks. Not liking the sound of that. Not liking it one measly bit.

"What do you mean *if you remember correctly*?" I studied him closely, trying to find some kind of tell, some kind of giveaway nervous tick, twitching eye, jerking knee, something. But other than that odd chewing of his bottom lip, I got nothing. He was stone-faced. Completely unreadable. Unwilling to give anything away. "You mean you've been here before, right?" I continued to probe, knowing he was hiding something, something I might very much need to know, for future use if nothing else, and I was determined to make him spill. "Was it for the Radiant Boy? Were you sent here to convince him to move on? And if you were, does that mean you *failed*? Does that mean you were unable to—" I raised my hands, curling my fingers into air quotes when I said, "*coax and convince* the ten-year-old to cross the bridge?"

He looked at me, his eyes betraying nothing when he said, "It's a long story, Riley. One we clearly don't have time for if you want to make it to London." And even though his voice was curt, and more than a little dismissive, it didn't

work. I was on to him now. I could feel it in my nonexistent bones.

He'd failed, where I was about to conquer.

Ha! Some guide he was turning out to be.

"Fine." He sighed, giving a little, but only a little. "Let's just say you're not the first to have a crack at this kid. Many have tried over the last, uh, several hundred years. But that just means that the bar is set so incredibly low no one's expecting much from you now. Which is lucky, since ten bucks says you run out of there screaming the first second you lay eyes on him."

"Ten bucks?" I rolled my eyes, swinging my blond hair over my shoulder. "*Please.* I can manifest mountains of ten-dollar bills, as can you. You wanna bet for real, then bet me something that's actually *worth* something. Seriously, give me a little something to strive for here."

He squinted, lips lifting at the sides when he said, "How about that trip to London? You convince the Radiant Boy to move on, you get your trip. If not—" He shrugged, leaving the rest to hang there, though the meaning was clear.

But I just shook my head. We'd already decided I was going, all I had to do was get the job done in a timely manner. No way was he changing the rules now. Not after they'd already been set.

He turned away, trying to hide the smile that snuck onto

his face. The smile I didn't have to see to know it was there. By the time he turned back again it was gone, wiped away clean, and replaced by a look of deep skepticism when he said, "Fine, you don't run out of there screaming, you succeed where all others have failed, you actually get the Radiant Boy all the way across that bridge and I'll teach you how to fly to London, okay? There. How's that?"

And when he looked at me, it was clear he was proud of himself. So sure that it would never happen, that I'd fail miserably, and the whole thing would be off.

Which was fine by me. As the youngest in my family, I was used to being underestimated, and I loved nothing more than to prove everyone wrong.

"What about Buttercup? Can he fly too?"

Bodhi glanced between my dog and me and just shrugged.

"Fine," I said, tucking my hair back behind my ears, preparing for the battle ahead, figuring the rest of the details could be worked out later. "You got yourself a deal."

I followed alongside him as he headed down the hall, stopping abruptly when he said, "Well, this is it." He pointed toward a heavy, elaborately painted door just a few feet away. "The blue room. Home of your newfound friend."

"Home of a *ten-year-old*," I mumbled, shaking my head.

Just about to walk right through the door when Bodhi

reached toward me, his arm wavering, hovering, before he dropped it back to his side, rearranged his expression from serious to friendly, as he said, "Riley—"

I turned, catching a look of real, genuine concern glinting in his eyes.

"It's—it's not what you think. There's plenty more to the story. Stuff you should probably know about before you go in."

But I just sighed and rolled my eyes, figuring it was just another stalling tactic, or some kind of psych-out. Figuring he was pretty much willing to do anything at this point, to make sure he won this one and keep me from a flying lesson he was so clearly reluctant to give.

"He's a *ghost*. He's *ten*. He goes by a *bizarre name* that either is or isn't his fault—that's yet to be determined—and I need to convince him to *move on*," I said, uncurling a finger with each point made and still left with a thumb pressed against the center of my palm. "Seriously, how hard can it be? And what's the worst he can do? It's not like he can kill me, you know? So, now that that's settled, can I please have at him? I'd really like to cross this one off my list—I've got a flying lesson to get to."

Bodhi looked at me, a long, hard, conflicted stare. Then he shook his head and waved me away with his hand. Maybe mumbling some stuff about wishing me good luck, about how he'd be waiting right outside for me in case I needed any help—and maybe not.

I'd never know for sure.

I'd already moved on.

Buttercup and I were already on the other side of that door.

## 13

The first thing I saw when I entered that room was—

No, scratch that. First let me say what it *wasn't*.

It *wasn't* the Radiant Boy.

It also *wasn't* the blue room.

In fact, nothing in that room came anywhere near a color that anyone would ever refer to as *blue*.

If anything, what I'd entered was the yellow room.

A room so incredibly bright and yellow, just looking at it made my eyes hurt.

"Back so soon?" Bohdi called, lounging on the banister in that slouchy way of his, chewing on a long, green straw, like the kind they give you at Starbucks, instead of his bottom lip which he was chewing on just a few moments earlier. Looking me over carefully and seemingly not the least bit surprised to see that I'd caved so early in the game.

Only I hadn't caved.

Not even close.

If anything, I was totally on to him.

He was still trying to mind-game me. Going so far as to send me to the wrong room.

Some coach he was turning out to be.

But no biggie. It's not like I actually needed Bodhi's guidance anyway. I mean, what kind of help could he possibly provide when it was so painfully clear he was actually trying to sabotage me?

So afraid I'd succeed at where he so miserably failed, he'd stop at nothing to doom me.

*That's it,* I decided. As soon as I got back, the first thing I would do was find Aurora, or even one of the other Council members if she wasn't available, and I'd demand a new guide. Or, better yet, *I'd* become Bodhi's guide. And the first thing on my agenda would be to give him a head-to-toe makeover. Insist he ditch the glasses, the clothes, start over with the hair—and that was just for starters. Then, once that was settled, once he wasn't so completely embarrassing to be seen with, well, then we'd see . . .

"Sit tight. We're not out of here yet," I called over my shoulder as Buttercup and I made our way down the hall. "You sent me to the *wrong room*, as I'm sure you already know. But don't get up. You're gonna need all of your energy for that flight to London, so stay right where you are. It won't be long before I

track down this scary little ten-year-old and send him on to the Sweet *Here* After so that we can be on our way."

I poked my head through a long series of doors, and after spying a green room, a white room, and a pink room, I'd finally found it.

Not the Radiant Boy, mind you; from what I could see, he was nowhere to be found. But there was an abundance of blue. And I mean, lots and lots of blue. Like an ocean. Yard after yard of the same blue fabric used to make up the drapes, the pillows, the blankets, even the little antique couch-and-chair set, what I think is called a *settee*, was upholstered in the stuff, while the walls were painted in an almost identically matching hue.

Blue, blue, I was drowning in blue. And when I gazed over at Buttercup, who was busy sniffing all four corners and then some, I couldn't help but wonder how all those earlier rooms had looked to him. If being dead somehow cured him of that canine inability to see most of the colors in the spectrum.

But even though we were clearly in the right room, there wasn't a single ten-year-old Radiant Boy to be found. Nor was there anything that even remotely resembled one.

Aside from Buttercup and me, the room was completely cleared of all earthbound entities.

But that's the thing with ghosts. They don't always stick to one place like most people think. Sure they have their preferences and their steady routines, places they like to hang in more often than others where they repeat the same acts over and over again. But for the most part, they have no boundaries. They can go anywhere they want, whenever they want. It's all there for the taking. All they have to do is choose it. And I should know, I was once one of them.

Though that's not to say I was about to go on some kind of big hunt for him, 'cause from what I could tell, there were at least a hundred more rooms in the place. And since it was close to being nighttime, and since Bodhi had said something about the boy liking to scare the beejeemums out of people, I pretty much figured the best, most energy-efficient thing to do would be to just wait it out until the sun went down, the sky went dark, and he'd begin his nightly fright fest.

Because if there's one thing I knew for sure, it's that all ten-year-old boys were the same. Dead—alive—it didn't make the least bit of difference. They were all annoying, all disgusting, all of them royal pains in the bums who just loved to torment people. And from everything I'd heard, this one was no different.

I climbed up onto the big canopied bed that was situated so high they actually provided a little step stool to get onto it, arranged all the pillows just the way that I liked them, then patted the bedspread, inviting Buttercup to leap up and join me. Then we sat back and waited. Waited for so long we both fell into a nice, deep, soundless sleep.

Until someone had the nerve to crawl in beside us.

At first, when I felt the mattress kind of dip, shift, and roll, I was so deeply involved in my dream state I didn't really think much about it. But then, when the snoring started, coming at me from both sides, my eyes snapped wide-open, and I turned my head to the right to find a large, bushy-browed man practically vibrating with his own snores. And when I looked to the left, I was greeted by the sight of a slightly (but only slightly) less bushy-browed woman doing the same.

I was sandwiched.

Sandwiched between two rather sizable, loudly snoring people I'd never seen before.

And I was so discombobulated that, well, I couldn't help it—my mouth popped open and a long, loud scream jumped out. Instantly waking Buttercup who pointed his nose toward the ceiling and started howling and barking like mad. Peering at me with his ears all perked up, his tail thumping like crazy, as he awaited further instruction, sure that it was some kind of game.

Only it wasn't a game.

Not even close.

I'd been rudely awakened, and shaken to the core, but

more importantly I'd screamed so loudly, I could practically *see* Bodhi standing in the hall, doing a lame little victory dance, straw bobbing crazily in his mouth while he gave himself a high-five.

*"Great,"* I mumbled, patting Buttercup on the head, trying to get him to calm down again, even though I knew the sleeping couple couldn't hear us unless we wanted to be heard, and truth be told, most of the time not even then. It was the rare person who could truly tune in to the dead, though they did exist, of that I was sure. "That's just *great.*" I shook my head and slid out from between the snoring couple, wishing this radiating kid would just hurry up and show himself already so that I could cross him over and be done with all this.

I moved toward the dressing table and peeked at their stuff, trying to get a handle on just what they were doing here. Lifting the top off a bottle of cologne that smelled just like dead pine needles (blech), before sniffing from the perfume just beside it and inhaling a nasty combination of mothballs and old, dried-out shrubs (double blech). A scent so startlingly bad the bottle accidentally slipped from my fingers and landed with a horrifying thud.

Well, make that a series of thuds, as I watched, frozen in panic, as it tumbled across the floor with Buttercup chasing behind it.

I peered at the sleeping couple, knowing that even though

they couldn't hear us or see us unless we wanted them to, unless we tapped into their own energy supply in order to manifest before them, there was nothing to stop them from hearing the sound of an inanimate object crashing to the ground. And seeing the way they both shuddered and stirred, I knew that on some level they had heard it, but were determined to sleep through it.

I moved on to their overflowing suitcases, curious to see what kind of clothes they'd packed for their haunted castle weekend getaway, when Buttercup, still entranced with the perfume bottle, hit it with his paw so hard it went spinning across the room and slammed into the wall where it cracked into a million little pieces of foul-smelling shards.

"Good one, Buttercup." I shook my head and rolled my eyes at him. "Way to go." I sighed, watching as he tucked in his tail and bowed his head low, knowing he was in trouble and unwilling to come anywhere near me. And I was just about to manifest a leash, which I knew he would hate but was obviously becoming necessary, when I heard a click.

Followed by a soft whirring sound.

And then a nervously whispered:

*"Did you get it?"*

I glanced over my shoulder, clutching a white T-shirt featuring a picture of the Union Jack tightly in my hand, only to find myself face-to-face with the dynamic duo—otherwise known as the husband and wife team who'd sandwiched me earlier. The two of them dressed in matching his and hers forest-green sweatshirts, with the words PENNSYLVANIA'S OWN INTERNATIONAL GHOST BUSTERS written in a large, loopy white scrawl across the front.

The husband holding some kind of recording device that seemed to really excite him, while the wife held the camera with a noticeably shaky hand. Creeping toward my general direction, clearly bent on capturing live, streaming footage of—

Well—

*Me.*

Crouched down low, T-shirt still dangling from the tips of my fingers, knowing I'd just been caught in the embarrassing act of nosing through their belongings.

My eyes darted frantically, realizing the full scope of what was really going on—not only had I been caught peeping—I'd also been caught inadvertently haunting a haunted room I'd fully intended to, well, *de-haunt.*

And there was nothing I could do about it. No way I could leave. I was stuck right there in that blue room until I could find a way to accomplish what I set out for. Otherwise Bodhi would never let me fly to London, never let me hear the end of it.

"Buttercup!" I hissed, dropping the T-shirt and hearing

them both gasp at the sight of it seemingly falling through the air of its own accord. Determined to keep my voice to a whisper, but by the way they gaped at their recorder, at the little squiggles and lines that jumped all around, it was clear that even though they couldn't see me or hear me, their equipment registered every last bit. "Come here, *now!*" I called between gritted teeth, annoyed by the way he'd loped toward them, sniffing then licking their hands as though they were long-lost friends suddenly reunited again.

He slunk toward me, tail tucked tightly between his legs as his big brown eyes gazed into mine. "That's better," I cooed, scratching his head to show I was more annoyed than mad, watching as the couple lifted their hands and studied the fingers Buttercup had just slobbered all over, before turning to each other, bushy brows raised as if to say: *Did you feel that?*

"You need to stick by me, *not* them. No matter what happens from here on out, I need you by my side, okay? We can't take any chances—I just have to figure out what to do before they—"

The woman moved toward me, moved in small baby steps as she crept across the floor. Her large bare feet, riddled with corns and bunions, with nail polish so badly chipped they made my own nails look salon fresh. Raised up high onto her tippy-toes, padding across the rug, video camera held out before her, the soft whir of it the only sound in the room as it recorded what I could only assume were a series of white, glowy, wavering images of one smallish blob of light and one even smaller blob of light, since, from all the shows I'd ever seen on TV that covered ghosts and hauntings and such, it was pretty rare for those recorders to pick up anything more.

"He's not alone," she whispered, waving to her husband from over her shoulder. "There's someone with him, someone smaller, like they're crouched down low."

*He?*

I narrowed my eyes and scowled, nudging Buttercup even closer to my side. Tugging on my skirt and running my fingers through my hair until it was arranged a little more nicely, a little more girly, completely offended by the fact that I'd just been mistaken for a ten-year-old *boy*.

"Is it him? Is it really the *Radiant Boy*?" her husband called, the words rising at the end in a potent mix of excitement and fear.

"Yes," she said, her voice having firmly decided, though her eyes weren't quite as convinced. "At least it certainly seems like it. And he's got someone with him—someone smaller— there are *two* Radiant Boys here!"

*Oh brother.*

I rolled my eyes and shook my head, sitting back on my heels as she continued to creep closer and closer.

Some ghost buster she was turning out to be. Mistaking

what was clearly a cute blond girl and her adorable yellow Lab for not one, but two bratty little boy ghosts. *Sheesh!*

"Try to speak with them—try to make contact," her husband urged. His gaze was fixed on the screen of his little handheld device, eager to see the lines shift and move once again. "Ask him why they're here, and what they might possibly want. Ask them if they have any messages they might like to pass on." Saying all of that as though I could only hear the words if *she* said them. As though she had some special patented way of communicating with the dearly departed.

Her husband came up behind her, seizing the camera she passed over her shoulder and steadying it in one hand while keeping the voice recorder going in the other. Watching as his wife crept even closer, running her hands over her wrinkled green sweats while completely ignoring the bed hair that, had I been her, I would've been way more concerned about.

"Is there any message you'd like us to pass on? Is there anything we can do for you?" the woman asked, squatting down on her haunches, as her knees cracked so loudly and violently, I actually jumped in surprise. Cringing back against the wall as she angled her face until it was dangerously close to Buttercup's and mine.

"Yes," I said, finding my voice again and nodding sincerely. "I'd really like it if you could just pack up your equipment and move on, so I can deal with this Radiant Boy on my own.

You know, the one you actually *came* here to see? Seriously, move it along so I can finish the job."

I scowled, knowing she wasn't about to go anywhere. Not as long as Buttercup and I were inadvertently giving her the thrill of her ghost-busting lifetime, even though, technically speaking anyway, neither of us could truly be considered as earthbound entities, since we were only there on a mission, and therefore had no plans to stay—a small, but pretty substantial fact that was completely lost on her.

I sat back and sighed, long, loudly, no longer caring when she turned toward her husband, her eyes wide, head bobbing up and down as she said, "Did you feel that? Just now? That rush of cold air?"

He nodded, his gaze running the track between the camera's display, the voice recorder, his wife's crazy eyes, and back.

"Are you getting all this?" she asked, rising in a way that made her knees crack again, causing Buttercup to wince and me to cringe.

"All of it," he mumbled. "Every last bit of it." He smiled, his eyes shining brightly.

"Fantastic!" she exclaimed, face beaming, cheeks flushed with excitement, as her hair, still not attended to since she'd jumped out of bed, pretty much stood up on end.

And watching all of that, well, it was just too much.

Not only had I been recorded and filmed, destined for

some pathetically dorky, homegrown, schlocky, ghost-busting Web site, but I'd yet to see the Radiant Boy, and as long as they kept this up, it was clear that I wouldn't.

I slumped against the wall, and glared at the couple before me, hoping they'd get a good shot of *that* amongst the rest of their footage. Watching as they closed in on us, stopping just short of where Buttercup was crouching down low, transitioning into full-on guard dog mode, as he let off a low, menacing growl.

"Oh, now you decide you don't like her?" I looked at him, and shook my head. "What about earlier when you were slobbering all over her hands? Huh, what about that?"

But just after the words were out, I noticed she wasn't the one he was growling at.

There was someone behind her.

Someone creeping up behind both her and her husband.

Someone who glowed so brightly the whole room lit up.

Someone who could only be described as—

*Radiant.*

# 14

B ehind him, the room shook.

    Objects flew.

As the ghost-busting couple bolted through the door with Buttercup close on their heels. Dropping their equipment and abandoning their belongings without a second glance, the shrieking echo of the husband's high-pitched scream lingering in the air long after they'd left.

Leaving me to face the Radiant Boy all on my own, as practically anything and everything that wasn't nailed down or weighing in at over two hundred pounds went soaring through the air, directed solely at me.

A chair nearly sliced me in half.

A lamp nearly cut off my head.

As a pair of graying old tube socks with holes in both the toes and the heels lifted right out of the couple's suitcase and headed straight for my neck, completely bent on strangling me.

All of it whirling about in a frenzied gale-force wind that could rival any Midwestern tornado, and refusing to stop until the entire room and its contents were either broken, upended, or no longer anywhere near their original place.

I cowered against the wall, narrowly avoiding a rogue blow dryer that hissed and looped before me like a venomous snake. Too afraid to close my eyes in case I might miss something, too afraid to keep them open for what I might see. Squinting into the wind and debris at the Radiant Boy glowering over me, wishing I'd just grabbed hold of Buttercup's tail and sailed right out of there while I'd still had the chance.

But it was too late for that. My failure to run left me with no choice but to deal with it. If I'd any hope of making it to London, learning to fly, or even just having the courage to face Bodhi again, I'd have to stay put, no matter what came *at* me.

No matter what became *of* me.

The Radiant Boy towered menacingly, having grown three times his size in just a handful of seconds. The blond curls that had been springy and bouncy just a moment before morphed into angry, vicious, three-headed snakes, while his body emitted a glow so bright—so *radiant*—it was all I could do not to cover my face. As his eyes raged ominously, two fiery, flaming pits of anger focused on me—though it was nothing compared to his mouth—an infinite black hole—a bottomless abyss—gaping so wide I had the unmistakable feeling he intended to swallow me completely.

I clamped my mouth shout, desperate to keep the scream from escaping. My eyes locked on those two flaming pits as he moved closer and closer still, knowing he was the scariest thing I'd ever seen in both my life and death combined. And that includes my worst nightmares, shows on TV, and even the movies I wasn't allowed to watch but did anyway.

Nowhere had I ever seen anything quite as frightening as he.

His fiery eyes raging in a way so intense I could actually feel their white-hot scorching heat, as the infinite void of his mouth practically sucked the air right out of the room. Knowing only one thing for sure:

No trip to London could ever be worth it.

And as for flying, well, it was clearly overrated.

But just as I turned, sneaking one foot halfway through the wall, eager to make my escape—I thought about Bodhi.

Thought about the smirky look he'd surely give me the second he found me in the hall, all wide-eyed and scared witless.

I thought about *failing*, and just how awful that always makes me feel.

And I knew I couldn't do it.

Couldn't allow myself to cave quite so easily.

Not without putting up a good fight at least.

No matter what would become of me, no matter what that Radiant Boy tried to do, I had to see it through.

I spun on my heel and placed my hands on my hips, squaring my shoulders as I narrowed my gaze and screwed up the courage to say, "Just what is it that you're trying to prove here, anyway?" Hoping he couldn't see the way my limbs all trembled and shook.

He crept closer, eyes glowing like crazy, mouth gaping wider—wider than I ever would've thought possible—as he closed the gap between us with surprising speed. Those angry, hot orbs practically singeing the brows off my face as he leaned toward me and shook the snakes loose from his head. Freeing hundreds of slimy, red-eyed, three-headed, angrily snapping snakes with razor-sharp fangs—all of them slithering, wriggling, and writhing toward me.

I sprang toward the settee, balancing myself on the slick marble-topped table as the snakes slid all around. Their numbers multiplying so quickly they completely obliterated the smooth, polished wood floor that had been there just a moment before—morphing it into a bottomless, hissing sea.

And even though I tried to stay calm, tried to remind myself that I was already dead, that they couldn't really hurt me no matter how much they tried, it was no use. There was no overcoming my fear.

A sea of snakes with no escape.

It was pretty much my very worst nightmare come true.

Or, at least that's what I thought until the flaming-eyed, snake-haired, demon-faced Radiant Boy morphed into something far worse.

Transforming himself into a completely crazed circus clown with huge red shoes that bounced right over the snakes, stirring them into a wild, lashing frenzy as he leered at me with his creepy, exaggerated face. His oversized, sloppy red mouth a jagged gash in his flesh, dripping thick rivulets of blood all down his front, as the flames continued to burst from his eyes.

He leaned toward me, allowing the frenzied, snapping snakes to slither up and down his arms, and I was just about to bolt, just about to cry "uncle" and get myself to safety, no longer caring about what Bodhi might do, no longer caring about anything but freeing myself of this beast, when I found that I couldn't.

Couldn't move.

Couldn't run no matter how hard I tried.

Somehow, entirely against my will, and without my even realizing it, I'd been strapped and harnessed into what I soon recognized as a dentist's chair.

I opened my mouth to scream, hoping to alert Bodhi, Buttercup, the ghost-busting couple, *someone—anyone—* knowing I needed all the help I could get. Clamping it shut the second I saw the horrifying assortment of drills and picks and needles he wielded before me—leaving me no choice but to silence myself.

And that's when I realized what was truly going on.

This scary, sadistic, completely crazy, drill-wielding, snake-charming, orthodontist/clown/Radiant Boy had seen right through me. Right into the very heart and soul of me.

He'd tapped into my very worst fears.

Snakes—three-headed ones at that!

Clowns—stemming from that horrible summer day at the Oregon Country Fair, when I was just a little kid and some crazy mime/clown got all up in my face and refused to stop following me, stop mocking me, until my dad was forced to intervene.

Dental instruments—an approved form of torture, I'd no doubt about that.

But what I didn't know was how he managed it—how he'd read me so well.

And it terrified me to think of just what else he might know.

His flaming eyes and bleeding mouth veering closer and closer as a tangle of snakes leapt onto my chair causing me to cringe, squishing back in my seat as far as I could, wishing I could scream, find a way to call for help, but knowing that to do so would only allow admittance to those horrible,

whirring instruments. Pressing against the thick canvas straps, struggling against them with everything that I had. But it was no use.

He'd already won.

I was well on my way to joining the ranks of every Soul Catcher who'd come before me and failed.

# 15

I ground my teeth together and squinched my eyes shut, unwilling to see any more. Cursing Bodhi under my breath for putting a rookie like me in a situation like this with virtually no warning, no proper training of any sort, and cursing Buttercup as well for abandoning me in what was clearly a time of deep need.

And I was just about to do it, just about to beg him to stop, to tell him that for all I cared he could haunt this place for the next hundred years, when he emitted a roar so loud, I couldn't help but peek. Couldn't help but peer into that creepy wreck of a face, watching in terror as it transformed from crazy flaming-eyed clown to every horror movie monster of the last thirty years.

And that's when I knew:

*He didn't know me at all!*

Hadn't tapped into the deepest part of me like I'd thought.

He was merely tapping into all the usual fears—the ones most of us shared.

And the only thing keeping me here, scared out of my wits and chained to that chair, was my *belief* that he had some kind of power over me.

My belief that the flying furniture could've harmed me, when clearly it would've just passed right through.

My belief that I couldn't overcome the snakes and the dental instruments—that they were bigger than me, too powerful to fight.

When the truth is they weren't.

And neither was he.

Not in the least.

And realizing that, well, it didn't make the snakes go away, didn't make the dental drills disappear, but it did make me stronger—strong enough to conquer my fears. So by the time he reached his arms toward me and threw back his head—well, I didn't cringe.

In fact, I didn't do much of anything at all.

I just calmly unbuckled all the harnesses and straps as I watched the Radiant Boy—*falter.*

Falter in a way that set him completely off balance.

Falter in a way that somehow—*split him into three!*

I sat there, mouth hanging open, a fresh unheard scream tickling the back of my throat, thinking the only thing scarier

than one angry Radiant Boy—was half a six-pack of angry Radiant Boys.

But only when they were all grouped into a pyramid like they were just before the fall. After losing their balance and tumbling to the ground, well, there was no doubt that I was in charge now.

I slid off the chair and cleared the floor of snakes simply by *wishing* for them to be gone. Then jutting my hip and tossing my hair over my shoulder, I cocked my head to the side and said, "So, you work as a team." I nodded, pausing for a moment to take them all in. "Well, I guess that explains why no one's been able to convince you to move on all these years. You've probably spent the last several centuries either working in shifts, or ganging up on people in your big scary pyramid maneuver. Not quite a fair fight when you think about it, now is it?"

They scrambled to their feet, trying to assume a tough-guy pose but it was too late. Two of them choosing to hang back, as one of them stepped forward as their leader, and I couldn't help but wonder why they'd chosen him since they all seemed pretty much the same to me. But as he drew closer, as all of them drew closer, I saw that they weren't the same at all.

When they were all bunched up, piled high on top of each other and pooling their energy, they took on that same, bright, radiant glow. But, taken in separately and individually, well, they had some very distinct differences. One was tall, one not so tall, and one more or less medium, and while two had hair that could best be described as platinum in color, the one who stepped forward was more of the strawberry blond variety, and he's the one who chose to lift his shoulders, puff up his chest, tilt his chin high, and address me.

"I command you to leave," he said, voice steady and strong and more than a little intimidating.

And even though the visions of snakes and the crazy clown wielding dental instruments were still fresh in my mind, I had no choice but to move past it, just clear it out completely. If I was to get anywhere with them, make any progress at all, it was imperative I show them I wasn't that same scared little ghost girl from a moment ago.

"Please tell me you're not serious," I said, knowing I might be pushing it, but still. Even though there were three of them and only one of me, they were still only a bunch of ten-year-olds, which, in my mind, pretty much made me the boss of them. "I mean, you're not serious about *commanding me*—are you?" I gazed all around, noting every little detail as I vowed to remember this exact moment. What the room looked like, what *they* looked like, knowing it would become one of my favorite parts to retell later. I shook my head, correctly reading the sudden burst of flames in his eyes as outrage, when I said, "Oh boy, it looks like you *are* serious. Okay." I nodded,

trying not to cringe at the sight of it. "But see, here's the thing, I *can't* leave—or at least not yet. I've got a job to do—and—well—I'm not going anywhere until it's done. So, it seems like we've got ourselves a little problem, I mean, what with your *commanding* me and all."

He glanced over his shoulder and looked at the others, receiving two halfhearted shrugs for his efforts, but still, it was enough for him to face me again and say, "I pronounce you to be gone! You must leave at once!" He lifted his arms, palms facing up as more three-headed snakes slithered down them and sprang toward me.

But I just batted them away, knowing they were only as real as I allowed them to be. In the big scheme of things, there was nothing he could do to hurt me.

I shrugged my shoulders and made for the blue uphol-stered settee. Turning the chair back onto its feet, and plop-ping myself upon it. Correctly assuming this was going to take a little longer than I'd hoped, what with all the *commandments* and *pronouncements* I'd be expected to get through, so I may as well make myself comfortable.

He stood before me, reddish-blond brows merged over the angry red orbs that stood in for his eyes. But I didn't react, I refused to give him that. And then after a few more demands, a few more decrees, and a whole slew of urgently stressed proclamations, he switched off.

In fact, they all switched off.

So that they no longer glowed, were no longer red eyed, and a trio of normal pink mouths replaced the bottomless black holes that had recently stood in their place.

Looking pretty much like any other gang of ten-year-old boys as they stood there before me. Well, except for the truly dreadful, completely unbelievable, wish-you-could've-seen-it-for-yourself, *awful* matching white short suits with the matching white kneesocks and shiny, black shoes.

And I couldn't help but hope those had been the clothes they'd been buried in, because if they'd chosen that ensemble on their own, well, I wasn't sure I could ever get through to them.

"Why aren't you afraid of us?" the one I was beginning to think of as strawberry head asked.

I shrugged, taking a moment to look him over before I said, "Well, if it makes you feel any better, at first I clearly was. I mean, you saw the way I almost took off. And then with that whole killer clown thing with the drills and the picks—" I shuddered at the memory of it. "Well, you nearly did me in! But when you started with all the scary monster stuff, well, let's just say it was pretty much a dead giveaway." I smiled, adding, "Pun intended," really cracking myself up. But when they didn't join in, I was quick to add, "Anyway, that's pretty much what did it. I mean, most of those movies were way before my time, and that's pretty much the moment I knew."

"Knew what?" He pressed his lips together, looking me over in that creepy way that only a ten-year-old can.

"Knew that you were counting on the fact that I'd be too scared to realize I'm in control—that *I'm* the one who allows the fear to win. And that my refusal to feed it, to let it take over, would diminish its power over me—*your* power over me." I nodded, and, even though I tried not to, I couldn't help it, a triumphant smile crept across my face. Which only seemed to annoy him even more. "Not to mention the fact that I'm already just as dead as you, so there's really not much else you could do to hurt me, now is there?" I added.

"Oh, we could do plenty! We could—" The blond one on the left piped up, rushing forward and shaking his small fist in the air, until strawberry head turned and flashed his palm, sending him slinking right back to his place again.

"We're not leaving if that's what you're here for. Plenty of others have tried, you know. And trust me, I mean *plenty*. But we're still here. Have been for hundreds of years. So, maybe *you're* the one who should move on, because we've no plans to stop. And if you continue to insist, well, it'll just end up being a big fat waste of your time."

"Maybe." I shrugged, my fingers picking at a loose thread on one of the blue cushions, acting as though I was only mildly invested in this, as though I had nothing important riding on it. "But then again, maybe not." I raised my gaze until it met his. "I mean, did it ever occur to you that maybe you guys are the ones wasting your time? Seriously, think about it. Hundreds of years spent running around in outdated little short sets just so you could get your jollies by scaring the beejeemums out of ghost-seeking tourists." I shook my head. "Hundreds of years of the same lame routine." I sighed, making a point to look at each of them. Just the thought of it seemed exhausting and pointless. "And for what may I ask? What could possibly be the point of all that? And just what exactly do you get out of it, anyway? I mean, *really*? Don't you ever feel like taking a little *vay-kay*, or even a week-long break?"

"We *do* take breaks! We work in shifts I'll have you know!" shouted the other blondie.

But shifts or no shifts, they weren't getting it, weren't getting it at all. I'd spent twelve full years bugging my older sister to the point of, well, complete and total *ridiculousness*. But still, that was nothing compared to the colossal waste of the last few centuries they'd committed to. Talk about a time suck.

"My point is—" I clutched the cushion to my chest for a moment before tossing it aside. Making sure I had their full attention before I went on to add, "What's the payoff?

Seriously. Why bother with the flaming red eyes, gaping black holes, and—and all of *this*?" I motioned toward them, drawing an invisible line from the top of their curly heads all the way down to their immaculately shined shoes.

And that's when the other one finally spoke, standing just to the right of strawberry head when he said, "What's the *payoff*?" His bright blue eyes met mine, looking at his friends as they snickered and laughed amongst themselves. "*Fame*. That's what. Worldwide *fame* is the payoff." They shook their heads and rolled their eyes, smirking at me as though I was a grade-A moron.

I squinted, unsure I'd heard right. I mean, there was no way they could be serious about that.

"We're *famous*," he repeated, his voice as determined as the expression on his face. "We have *name recognition*. People come from all over the world just to try to get a glimpse of us—a chance to photograph us—to catch a voice recording of us—to have an encounter with us—to tell their friends back home they lasted through the night with us—" He glanced at his buddies as they all burst out laughing, his eyes back on mine when he said, "Which, by the way, is a big fat lie since no one's ever made it through the entire night in this room. *No one.* No exceptions." His face grew stern. "And, let's not forget about all the books, and articles, and TV shows about us. *We're famous.* International superstars! And we have been for years. We're like—we're like the Backstreet Boys in a way—only dead."

*Oh boy.* Suddenly, I couldn't help but feel bad for them for not only being completely delusional, but tragically outdated as well. I mean, *the Backstreet Boys*—could they have picked a more ancient reference? I shook my head and looked them over. They reminded me so much of some of the kids I used to go to school with, whose sole ambition was to be famous. For what? They hadn't a clue. All they knew is they were destined for the spotlight.

And their first stop was YouTube.

My eyes grazed over them. They were so indignant, so sure that what they were saying was true, and I knew I had to find a way to break it to them.

I cleared my throat, taking a deep breath purely out of habit before I went on to say, "Um, I hate to break it to you, but you're nothing like the Backstreet Boys. Not to mention, how do you even know about the Backstreet Boys anyway? You live in a castle in the middle of nowhere."

They stared at me, a united front of white suits, white kneesocks, and outraged red cheeks.

"You're not the first to look through people's belongings, you know. We have access to computers, we've checked out an iPod or two," said the smallest blond kid, as his buddies

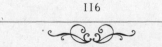

all snickered and laughed, taking a moment to shake their heads at me.

"Just because we live *in a castle in the middle of nowhere* doesn't mean we don't know the same stuff you do," strawberry head added.

I nodded. I didn't see that coming, I'll give them that. To think that any ghost would be in touch enough to know about boy bands of the last decade and yet still choose to dress like that was beyond me. But then again, look at Bodhi—an almost-pro skater dude who for whatever reason chose to dress like a dork. People were complicated—both the living and the dead, of that I was sure.

"Okay, fine. My bad. I'm sorry I misjudged your knowledge of pop music. Still, I'm sorry to say, but you're nothing like the Backstreet Boys. Because the truth is, millions of people all around the world *loved* them, but—well—how many people *love* you?"

I watched as they exchanged bewildered gazes, their thoughts of confusion and despair like a vibrating rumble that flowed through the room.

Then strawberry head shook his head firmly, determined to take charge and regain control once again, saying, "Do *not* listen to her. None of it's true! She's messing with us. It's part of her mission or whatever agenda she has." He shot me a scathing look that was almost as bad as when the flames shot from his eyes. "The point is, maybe they don't exactly *love* us—but they *love* to fear us. People come from all over the world just because of *us*! Without us, Warmington Castle would be ruined! Nobody would bother to visit. It couldn't continue and would shut down for sure." The blonds both nodded, two sets of bobbing heads flanking him on either side.

"Maybe—maybe *not*." I frowned, knowing that could very well be true though it was pretty much irrelevant here. "But what's it to you either way? I mean, are you getting a cut of the share? Is anyone actually *thanking* you for volunteering to work here? All that time you spend, all the long hours you put in—what's the payoff? Seriously, did it ever occur to you that you're totally being used? Taken advantage of in the very worst way? You guys give a whole new meaning to the term *graveyard shift*. And really, other than your questionable claim to fame, what's in it for you?"

They looked at each other, thoughts murmuring back and forth in a swirl of static and sound.

"Look," I said, smoothing my skirt as I stood from my seat and approached them. "Here's the deal. I know you're afraid of being nobodies, of being invisible—of no one even remembering that you ever did exist. And trust me, I know exactly how you feel because back when I was still alive, I was afraid of the same exact thing. And I wasted so much

time—my whole entire life really—just following my older sister around, trying to be just like her. To me, she was important, *hugely* important. She was pretty and popular and, well, she was somebody special. And I was sure that if I could be just like her, mimic her in just the right way, then I could be somebody special too. But the truth is, trying to be like Ever didn't make me important or special—it just made me an annoying tagalong. And maybe even a little bit of a brat."

I looked at each of them, hoping my words were beginning to penetrate in some way. "What I'm trying to tell you is that you have a choice. You can either stay here and continue to scare the beejeemums out of people, or you can move on to someplace that's—well—" I hesitated, not wanting to lie and say it was *better*, since I pretty much knew that wasn't entirely true. But still, needing to say something, I said, "Someplace that's *new*. And—*different*. And far more exciting than anything you have going on here." I motioned around a room so upended it looked like a rugby match had just taken place, remembering the manifesting, the beaches, the everchanging, glorious Here & Now scenery, and knowing that much was true. "I really think you'll like it there. You just need to give it a chance, that's all." Stopping just after the words were spoken, and wondering if maybe that last bit of advice applied to me too.

"But what if we *don't* like it there? What if we get there and decide that we hate it and we'd rather be *here*?"

I looked at them, tempted to lie to get this thing over with. To tell them they wouldn't miss the earth plane, not even the slightest, tiniest, most minute bit.

But I couldn't.

Couldn't dupe them like that.

So instead, I looked them each in the eye and said, "The thing is, you *will* miss it. I'm afraid there's just no getting around it, it's practically guaranteed. But, if you play it right, you could come back for a visit. I mean, look at me—I'm here, *right*? Not to mention all the others before me who came here to get you. So, what do you say? Are you ready for an adventure, to try something new for a change?"

They turned to each other and consulted among themselves. Taking their time to go over it thoroughly, point by point, before turning back to me. Strawberry head taking the lead once again when he said, "Is now the time when you make the light appear?"

But I just laughed, shaking my head as I said, "No, silly. Now's the time when I take you to the bridge."

# 16

If I'd had one of those special cameras like the ghost-buster lady's, I would've used it to take a picture of Bodhi's face when I exited the blue room with a whole string of (not-so) Radiant Boys behind me.

"So, what now?" I asked, as they milled all about. Narrowing my eyes and shaking my head at Buttercup who'd run toward me and was busily licking my fingers as he gazed up at me with those big brown eyes, desperate for me to forgive him for bailing on me, and attempting to get on my good side again. "How do we get them to the bridge?"

But Bodhi didn't answer.

He was far too speechless for that.

His gaze darting among them, counting and recounting in his head, obviously newly amazed each time it added up to three.

"How did you——" He shook his head and removed his

glasses, rubbing his eyes and blinking a bunch of times, before putting them back on and blinking some more.

"Never mind how I did it, just tell me how to get these guys to the bridge before they chicken out and change their minds," I said, refusing to give away my tricks of the trade, not while I was still learning my way.

"Who you calling a chicken?" strawberry head said, making his eyes and mouth go all creepy again, in a way that made Buttercup whimper and Bodhi almost fall off the banister.

But I just looked right at him and said, "*You*. I'm calling *you* a chicken. Ten bucks says you and your friends cry like babies and refuse to even cross it."

"You forget that money has no value to us. Or, maybe you didn't forget." Strawberry head lifted a brow and smiled knowingly. "You don't need to trick us into crossing over, you know. Your little speech was convincing enough."

"Really?" I tried to hold back my smile, but it was no use. I couldn't help but feel proud of myself, and proud of them for making the choice that they had. "Well, the truth is, you helped me too." *As much as three ten-year-olds can help an older, wiser, more mature girl of twelve.* "So, well, thanks."

"You're welcome," strawberry head said, suddenly sounding far more mature than his years. "And, for the record, just so you know, we're almost eleven. Oh, and my name's not strawberry head." His eyes met mine but thankfully they bore no ill will. "It's Hans. And this is Dieter and Wolfgang." He motioned toward his blond brothers. We're triplets, and I'm the oldest—by seventy seconds."

I nodded, feeling bad that he'd clued into my thoughts. I was really going to have to watch myself if I wanted to make any friends in the afterlife.

"So? Just where is this bridge anyway?" Wolfgang said, as his brothers nodded beside him, obviously eager to move on to the next adventure.

Bodhi slid his straw to the other side of his mouth, fully recovered from the shock of seeing them and completely back on his game when he said, "Okay, now everybody join hands. And Riley, you hold on to Buttercup, as we all imagine a shimmering veil of soft golden light . . ."


The trip to Summerland was brief. So brief it included no time for looking around, reconnecting with friends, or getting reacquainted with my favorite old haunts.

It's like, one minute we'd walked through the golden mist, landed smack-dab at the foot of the bridge, and were bidding the Radiant Boys farewell, and the next, we were right back where we left off. Standing in the long hallway in

Warmington Castle, as I looked at Bodhi and said, "Do you think they'll be reunited with someone—like maybe their mother? Or has it been too long for all that?"

But Bodhi just shrugged, dismissing me and my question in a way so noncommittal, so completely uninterested, it immediately got on my nerves.

I mean, a little credit would've been nice.

A little: *Way to go! Good job!* Even a high-five would've sufficed.

But *nooo.*

Not only had he barely even acknowledged the monumental task I'd just pulled off, but he also managed to land us right back where we started, which wasn't anywhere close to London, or a runway for that matter.

"What gives?" I scowled, wondering why he made us come all the way back here.

I'd done what I'd set out to do, completed my task and successfully rid the place of its ghosts—all three of them at that. And as far as I was concerned, now that I'd won the bet, it was time not only for my flying lesson, but also my trip to London.

It was clearly stated in the terms of our earlier agreement.

It was as simple as that.

And no way was I letting Bodhi find some kind of loophole to shirk his way out of our deal.

No way was I letting him get away with something as unfair as that.

But Bodhi just looked at me, his shoulders hunched, gaze sheepish, green straw bobbing up and down between his teeth when he said, "Um, I might not have mentioned it earlier, but there's more. Just one more thing to take care of, and then we're out of here. I promise."

"What do you mean *one more thing*?" My hands clutched at my hips, as I made sure both my face and voice displayed just how completely furious I was. "You can't just go expanding my job description like that! It's *not fair*! I did exactly what I was supposed to and I got it done pretty quickly if I do say so myself. So, why the delay? Let's go already! Seriously. Let's move it! I want to be soaring over the River Thames by sunrise—*or else*!" I scowled, having no idea what the *or else* part actually stood for, but still, there it was. Besides, fair's fair, and I was determined to see that the already clearly established set of rules were not only abided by, but *met*.

Feeling more than a little confused when Bodhi looked at me and said, "This one's not for you, Riley. This one's for me."

## 17

Apparently, as it turned out, Bodhi, my guide/teacher/ coach/counselor/boss had his own guide/teacher/ coach/counselor/boss, who, as it also turns out, was less than enthusiastic with the job Bodhi had done so far.

Even though he'd pretty much started his day being summoned to the stage in what I learned had been a sort of graduation ceremony, he still had plenty more to accomplish.

Plenty more to live up to—so to speak.

Or at least that was the gist I was able to take away from his rambling litany of hazy, vague, purposely ambiguous mumblings. Carefully guarding any and all of the details, and refusing to share them with me.

And trust me, I was lucky to even get that much. Because when I started to hound him for more, wanting to know just who exactly his guide was, if it was possibly one of the Council members, or maybe even somebody else—and just what exactly his own job description might be—what was truly expected of a guide—and what were the consequences for those who failed at their tasks—what would happen to him if he failed to help me learn and grow and better myself—he clammed up.

And when I continued to press on to what I really and truly wanted to know—which was why he was looking and acting so freaked at just the mere *thought* of the task that awaited him—he turned away completely.

Just shut down, refused to speak, and showed me his back.

Giving me the stoop-shouldered silent treatment.

Refusing to divulge anything more than he already had.

And when I gave up on the questions and decided to offer my assistance instead (anything to make it to London by daybreak I figured), he just shook his head and said, "This one's all mine. It's absolutely imperative I do it on my own."

*Great.* My face dropped into a frown as I snuck a quick peek at the grandfather clock in the hall, knowing that if this task, whatever it may be, took anywhere near as long as mine did, I wouldn't get to London 'til nightfall, if then.

"Listen." I smiled, knowing my motivations weren't exactly pure, were far too self-serving to ever be mistaken for altruistic, but still continuing on when I said, "I'm a trainee, *right*? And it's your job to—well—train me, *correct*?"

He nodded in his usual, noncommittal way, head bobbing

forward ever so slightly but just enough for me to translate it as a yes, if only to make things easier and get it moving along.

Slinking around to his side and watching as he continued to chew on that same dented-up straw when I said, "So, with that in mind, what better way to train me, than to allow me to watch the master—meaning *you*—at work? What better way for me to learn something new than to watch, firsthand, how it's done? And maybe—just maybe—get a little *hands-on* experience as well? But only if permission to do so is granted by you, of course," I added quickly, seeing the way his mouth sort of slammed down at the sides when I got to that last part. "So? Tell me, what do you say? Surely your guide can't fault you for that—for letting me watch you do your thing and complete your task?"

Bodhi looked at me, clearly weighing the pros and cons in his mind. Then, squinting down the long hall, he sighed and said, "Fine. But just remember, you asked for it."

# 18

He led us down the hall, far away from the blue room where I'd completed my task, and down the stairs, across a large foyer, and up another set of stairs, which led to yet another long hall, a smaller set of stairs, and a very narrow corridor with a tiny door at the very end that would require most people to stoop down low to get through, but not us, and onto still more stairs, until, at last, we were entering one of those turrets. One of those pointy tower-like things known to all the best castles that I'd always wanted to see the inside of.

But just as I started to rush the door, eager to manifest some seriously long, blond hair so I could have my long-awaited, much anticipated, *Rapunzelesque* moment, Bodhi stretched his arm across, barring me from going any farther when he said, "You sure about this?"

*Please.* It was all I could do not to roll my eyes in his face. Here I'd just faced down three glowing radiant brothers with red orbs for eyes and deep, dark, cavernous mouths, and he wanted to know if I *could handle it*? I mean, seriously, it was almost insulting. Just how bad could this possibly be?

"Because there's no shame in being scared," he said, studying me carefully, still chewing on that dumb straw, really working it into submission. "No shame at all. It's perfectly natural and I won't judge you if you decide to turn back while you still can. You've already proven yourself. You went in and succeeded where many before you have failed. You know, you're pretty amazing, Riley Bloom. You're the best Soul Catcher I've ever seen and it's only your first day out! But this is *my* task, not yours. And trust me, there's a reason for that."

I couldn't help it. For someone with a tendency to seek out all the compliments I could ever possibly get, the truth was, I wasn't always so great at receiving them. And just after he said all of that my eyes started to burn as a lump took over my throat, and it was all I could do to nod and look away. I was so humbled and embarrassed by his praise.

"Okay," I said, my voice hoarse, nearly a whisper. "But at least let me try, *please*. I'm eager to learn as much as I can."

He looked at me, his eyes searching my face before he nodded in consent. And the second he opened the door I heard it.

In fact, all of us heard it.

Including Buttercup.

This low, awful, moaning/wailing type sound.

The sound of despair.

The sound of someone so lost in their grieving, they could no longer function, no longer do anything but emit a noise that rang of nothing but death.

It was continuous. Unceasing. Going on and on and on in a way that felt like forever.

In a way that definitely gave me the creeps.

Bodhi looked at me and I at him, our gaze holding for a moment before he slipped right in front of me and climbed the set of steep narrow steps, as Buttercup and I trudged up behind him.

And when we got to the top, I saw her. Though I have to admit it actually took me a moment to really focus and zoom in to just exactly where the noise was coming from. Because even though it probably sounds weird, it was like she was so old, so gray, so faded, and so washed out, she practically blended right into those old, gray, faded, and washed-out walls.

Like she'd been in that room for so long, she'd started to resemble it.

To become a part of it.

Like a solid piece of heavy old furniture that's never been moved from its place.

I slunk back, clinging to the farthest wall as Bodhi approached her. Knowing that if I'd still been alive I'd be holding my breath in absolute horror, terrified to think of what might come next.

But, as it was, I was frozen in place. The bundle of energy that normally comprised the new, dead, ghostly version of me had come to a screeching halt as I hovered in place, with Buttercup crouched down beside me.

But no matter how close Bodhi crept, the woman remained totally and completely oblivious of his presence, unaware that we'd even entered the room.

She stood there, pressed up against the wall in a way so close, so seamless, it was like she was part of it. Appearing small and trim, her back curved as her narrow shoulders hunched forward, rising occasionally when a spasm of fresh tears overtook her, then dropping back again, falling well below the usual place. Her long cotton dress clinging to her in a series of unflattering, soaking wet clumps, everything about her so bland, so lackluster, so nondescript, the only thing that stood out, the only thing of any color was her hair. It was long, wavy, and dark, swept up into a careless bun that was barely held together by two pearl-tipped pins.

The three of us watched as she continued to stand there, peering out of a small, square window, grieving over something none of us could fathom, much less see.

Listening as the wailing continued, refusing to let up for even a second. It just went on and on and on, the sound of it

so heartbreaking, so disconcerting, so disturbing, so discombobulating, even Buttercup sank all the way down to his belly, rested his chin flat against the old stone floor, and placed a paw over each ear in a desperate attempt to avoid it.

And honestly, the second I saw that, I came *this* close to doing the same. Stopped only by Bodhi glancing over his shoulder, checking to see how we were doing, and not wanting him to know how completely freaked out and disturbed I was, I just waved my hand in the air, fluttering my fingers in a way that meant for him to not mind us, to just continue his business. Knowing that the sooner he got down to it, the sooner we could clear out of this small, stone, practically airless prison of sorts.

Only a handful of seconds in her presence and my Rapunzel fantasy was over, not to mention my previous fascination with castles and turrets and anything else of the sort. It was awful, small, dark, dingy, and damp and completely claustrophobic even for those of us that no longer breathed, and I couldn't even begin to see why anyone would choose to spend even a portion of their afterlife in such a horrible place, much less camp out here for hundreds of years.

The reasoning of some ghosts was beyond me.

Some of them just didn't make the slightest bit of sense.

Bodhi spoke to her, calling to her softly, quietly, and though I couldn't exactly make out the words, it was clear he

was trying to steal her attention, gain her trust, and convince her to turn around and face him. He even went so far as to remove those ridiculous glasses he wears, and place them in his inside pocket. Though I wasn't sure if it was so he could better see her, or so she could better see him—if she ever decided to turn around, that is.

Still, even though he looked a gazillion times better without them, the act alone pretty much amounting to one giant step away from total geekdom and one baby step toward, well, the opposite of geekdom—in the end, it's not like it made the slightest bit of difference, or at least not to her anyway.

She remained right there in place, rooted to her post. Still crying, still staring out the small, square window.

Oblivious.

Uninterested.

So lost in her grief, she had no idea she had company.

And watching her carrying on like that, well, I couldn't help but wonder if she ever got tired of it.

If she ever just stopped for a few minutes, and took a little break to at least wipe her eyes or blow her nose before she started up again.

Only to find out that she did.

And that the wailing would soon be replaced with something much worse.

# 19

She turned.

Turned and looked straight at us.

Or at least it seemed that way at first.

But right before I started to turn away, right before I shrank back in horror, tempted to grab hold of Buttercup and *vámanos* ourselves right out of there, never to return, I noticed that she wasn't *really* seeing us.

It was more like she was facing in our general direction, but her focus was inward, unable to see anything around her but the images she played over and over again in her head.

And when my gaze unwittingly, accidentally met hers— that was all I could see too.

I slumped down to the ground, whimpering, sniveling, feeling as though my plug had been pulled, as though my wick had been snuffed, and my bulb just burnt out. Sapped of all my energy as my arms instinctively circled around me, trying to protect myself against her pain, her fear, her loss, her complete and total agony—but it was no use. All I wanted to do was scream out, to join her in her chorus of grief, to wail, and moan, and pine, and cry in my own horrible, endless, unceasing way. But my throat was too lumpy, too hot, and it wouldn't allow anything to work its way in, much less find its way out.

And even though Bodhi was trying to shield me, raising his arms to block her from sight—it was too late.

Too late to look away.

Too late to do anything but continue to stare until I was completely immersed in her world.

Only Buttercup was smart enough to place his paws over his eyes and block her from view.

My gaze moved over her, noticing how even for a ghost, she was so unbelievably pale that the dark wisps of hair that'd broken free of her bun sprang against her face like a silhouette of tree branches caught in an unexpected blizzard of blinding white snow. While her dress, plain and high-necked, was made from a fabric that had clearly started out as black, but after centuries of being washed in an endless deluge of large, salty tears had weakened and faded until it was bleached the same color as the room. Though the constant flow of grief had wreaked far more havoc on her face than the fabric—corroding it into a series of deep, craggy

crevices where her cheekbones once rose, while forging bottomless valleys and gorges where her nose, lips, and chin
should've been. Reminding me in a strange, sick way of a trip
my family once took to the Grand Canyon, where my father
explained to Ever and me how the rise and fall of the water,
its incessant sway and lull, had the power to hone and carve
and completely obliterate parts of the rock like a finely honed
chisel.

The only part of her face that was even remotely recog-
nizable was the space where her eyes should've been.

Years of unceasing tears had washed them away until
there was nothing left but two matching, deep, dark, and
bottomless pools filled with murky black waters that sucked
me right in, until I was swirling and spinning, pulled deeper
and deeper—like water rushing down a drain, rainfall spill-
ing into a gutter, I was falling, flailing, and there was no way
to stop it.

No way to claw my way back.

No way to spare myself from her limitless grief.

I was drowning.

Fighting to keep my head above the dark, murky pool of
tumultuous, oily, swirling black waters that violently churned
all around me. Coughing and blinking and trying my best to
tilt my head back and just float, reminding myself to relax, to
stay calm, that panicking would just make it worse. Calling

upon everything I'd ever learned in every swimming lesson and junior lifeguard class I'd ever taken. Desperate to keep the water from flooding my lungs, even though deep down inside, I knew they didn't exactly exist anymore.

But it was too late.

Despite my attempts, despite my legs continuing to kick, despite my hands grasping and clawing, I couldn't overcome her. I was being pulled under. And for someone who just a few moments earlier didn't even breathe, I somehow knew that my very existence, not to mention my sanity, required me to hold on, to hang in there, to embrace the breath that now bubbled my cheeks, and to not let it go, no matter what became of me.

And just when I was sure I couldn't hold on any longer, a hand came out of nowhere, plunging straight toward me from somewhere above, as a voice called out to me.

A voice I immediately recognized as Bodhi's.

My fingers stretched toward his, as my legs furiously kicked, desperate to propel myself upward, vaguely aware of his fingers circling my wrist, and giving it a nice, firm tug that yanked me above the water, up to where there was oxygen, and air, and room still to breathe.

I gasped and sputtered, blinking that thick, oily water from my eyes, only to see Bodhi floating before me, his lips moving frantically as he said, "You have to stop looking. *Now!*

Turn toward the wall and she'll have no choice but to release you—it's the only way! Do it, Riley, do it now! *Please*."

But I didn't.

I didn't turn toward the wall.

And if you asked me why, well, at the time, I wouldn't have had an answer.

I guess some things are just automatic.

Instinctive.

Some things you just do, despite the fact that your entire being is shouting against it.

Some things just don't make any sense, until later.

Much later.

And this, as I would soon learn, was one of those things.

# 20

Bodhi was furious. Truly furious. Eyes narrowed and glaring at me as he shouted: "Dang it, Riley, I'm your *guide*, which means you *have* to do what I say!"

Which was soon followed by: "This is *exactly* why I didn't want to bring you here. This is *my* task, not yours. I'm the only one who can take care of this. So, for the last time, *please*, I'm *begging* you, *turn away*!"

But even after all that, I still didn't stop looking. I just stayed right there in place, floating, struggling to keep my head above water as the seas finally calmed down all around me, glad my dog had the good sense to sit this one out too.

"What's this about?" I asked, my voice sounding small, scared, and needy in a way that embarrassed me and aggravated him. "And where exactly are we right now? I don't get it."

Bodhi looked at me, his hair damp and clinging to his

cheeks, having lost his jacket in the current, and I couldn't help but hope that the nerd glasses had gone along with it.

"We're in her world now," he said, voice resigned like a sigh, clearly sick of arguing with me. "And it happens to be a dangerous one. One that is no place for children, and certainly no place for the faint of heart. So *please*, if you refuse to do what I ask, if you refuse to turn away and save yourself, then at the very least stay quiet. The water should stay calm now. Calm enough for me to leave you here on your own. But I'm warning you, Riley, no matter what happens next, no matter what you see or hear, *do not* head toward the rock. No matter how dire it may seem, you are much safer here. So please, just do what I say and stay put. Do *not* get involved no matter how bad things get. Okay? Can you do that for me?"

I nodded. Unsure if I could really follow through and keep a promise like that, especially if things really did get as bad as he seemed to think they would. Not to mention if the waters went all crazy and churning and scary again, then the rock would be the first place I'd head. But knowing he needed me to agree in order to get on with his task, I nodded my assurance, even though I wasn't sure if I could actually live up to my promise.

I watched as he floated away, cutting through the current as easily as a fish, before climbing onto what appeared to be a small, lonely island somewhere out in the distance, and what further squinting revealed to be a large, jagged rock jutting out from the sea.

And that's when I saw it.

And I'm pretty sure that's the same moment he saw it too.

The second he climbed up and secured himself there, we both watched, from our own separate vantage points, the exact cause of the ghost lady's anguish for the last several hundred years.

She was a murderer.

A child killer.

Or at least that's what everyone said.

Falsely accused of what was pretty much the worst crime a person could ever commit—that of killing her very own children.

Her three beloved sons, whom I immediately recognized as the golden-haired Radiant Boys I'd just crossed over a few moments earlier.

Only thing was—she was innocent. She'd done nothing of the sort.

She was merely a poor widowed mother left to take care of her sons on her own, forced to find work right here at the castle, and just naïve and innocent enough to trust the wrong person to look after her boys while she was gone.

A stable hand who promised to take them on a so-called fishing trip where instead of baiting a line, he drowned all three of them. Cleaning up nicely and planting just enough evidence to make it appear as though she'd done it—only to vanish nearly as soon as he'd come, never to be seen or heard from again.

And after being tried and punished with death, she took one look at the golden veil of shimmering light that led to the bridge, saw the way it glowed and swayed and beckoned for her, offering nothing but comfort and love and compassion and forgiveness—all of which she'd long been denied. But instead of joining it, instead of seeking the solace only it could provide—she turned her back, and chose instead to wander away. So driven by her overwhelming grief, her insurmountable blame, convinced she'd played a big part in it by being so naïve, by not looking after them properly, by not doing nearly enough to keep them all safe, she returned to the very scene where she first heard the news.

To the place where she stood looking for them, waiting for them to return . . .

And suddenly, just like *that*, I knew exactly where we both were.

We weren't so much in her *head* like I'd originally thought. Nor were we settled into a front-row center seat watching the memories she stored in her broken and damaged *heart*.

Nope.

Where we both were, Bodhi and I, was the darkest part of her *soul*.

The place she'd shut off from the world long ago. The place she'd condemned herself to. A self-imposed imprisonment for the last few centuries.

And now, like it or not, we'd joined her.

Were locked in with her.

And I had no choice but to watch as Bodhi braced himself against the rock, his arms spread wide, his head tilted back, his mouth open, as he started to take it all in.

Determined to swallow it—every last bit of the horrible grief that'd kept her chained to the earth plane for hundreds of years.

Determined to claim it for himself.

To steal it from her and make it his own.

# 21

Bodhi's body bucked and convulsed, as his eyes rolled back in his head. But when I started to swim toward him, he immediately stopped me in my tracks. Flashing his palm in warning, and telling me to stay back. Telepathically reminding me of the promise I'd made, that no matter how bad things got, I'd stay in my place.

This particular job was his, and I'd better not come any closer or interfere in any way.

So I shrank back, watching as his entire being continued to spasm, realizing he wasn't exactly fighting against it like I'd first thought. He wasn't battling against the tsunami of overwhelming grief he took in.

He was fighting against *her*.

Her refusal to rid herself of it.

To give it to him.

To unburden herself and move on.

It was like she'd stayed so long at that window, spent so many years crying, and moaning, and wailing her nonexistent heart out, she'd gotten to the point where she couldn't remember anything else.

Her grief had come to define her.

Without it, she feared she might cease to exist—completely disappear.

Unaware of how that very disappearance would actually be the best thing for her.

Sure, the sad, old version of her would fade away without a trace, but only so a new, improved, happier version could find a new life on the other side of the bridge.

I watched the struggle continue, knowing I had no right to interfere, that it was forbidden, that Bodhi wouldn't allow it. But still, that didn't mean I couldn't surround him with *hope*. Imagining the color in my mind as the most beautiful, radiant, rose-petal pink, I turned it into a giant, glistening bubble, and wrapped it around him as I held the wish near.

Eager for this to be over—for Bodhi to find enough strength to take it from her, release her from her grief, so that she could be free.

All the while trying not to think about what might become of him once he had swallowed her sorrow.

Where would it go?

Would he be forced to take her place at the window and wail for the next hundred years?

Or could he find a way to process it?

Treat it like they do with sewage and waste and gross stuff like that. Reconditioning it in a way where it's no longer toxic, no longer so completely destructive to live with.

And if he couldn't process it—if he couldn't treat it in some way—then what would become of *me*?

Would I ever find my way out of that bottomless sea?

Or would I be forced to tread in that black, oily water for the rest of eternity?

But still, even though all those thoughts were actively flooding my mind, I kept my promise, and I kept my place. Holding tight to that vibrant, pink bubble of *hope*, as my legs moved beneath me, and my arms spun in half circles by my sides. Watching as Bodhi continued to put up one heck of a fight, engaged in a battle of her dark, heavy soul versus his light.

Shaking and trembling, he struggled to consume all her pain, while I whispered to myself, over and over again, that it would all be all right. That the light always wins in the end. In all my favorite books, movies, and shows on TV— that's just the way it always goes.

Only this was all too real.

And like it or not, Bodhi and I were locked in this to-gether, our eternities depending on how this thing ended.

I closed my eyes, overcome with exhaustion, and not want-ing to see any more. Though I still clung to *hope*—hoping it might aid him in some small, acceptable way.

*Hoping* she would let go, give up the grief, and move on.

*Hoping* Bodhi would stay sure and strong and continue to fight.

And the next thing I knew, it was over.

Or at least my part was over.

I suddenly found myself outside of it all. Back in that small, dank room, watching from the sidelines as the ghost lady's dress whitened, her hair brightened, and the color re-turned to her cheeks in the way she must've looked before all the darkness moved in.

But the most remarkable change of all was her eyes.

The way they transformed from bottomless black oily pools—an endless sea of sorrow—to a calm brilliant blue.

And when she looked at me, looked right at me, her smile was so glorious, so luminous, so filled with *hope*, it just lifted her right up like a helium balloon as she sailed out that small window and up toward the sky.

I nudged Buttercup who was lying beside me, watching as he removed his paws from his eyes and immediately ran toward Bodhi who was curled up in the corner, arms circled

tightly around his waist, filled to the brim with grief and pain and no idea where to put it.

And all it took was one quick look at him to know that even though he appeared to be with us, he still really wasn't. Inside his head, inside his soul, he was back on that lonely rock island, fighting against the emotions he'd willingly taken on—trying to find a way to bear it, to process it, so that he too could release it and move on.

And while I wasn't sure if I was supposed to, and while I wasn't sure if it was permitted, and knowing there was a very good chance he might scold me later, I crept toward him. Kneeling down beside him as I placed my hand on his arm and streamed into his energy field. Having learned long ago, back when I was living in Summerland, that everything is made up of energy, our bodies, our thoughts, *everything*.

Which means that all of us are connected.

Which means that if we want to really know someone, or comfort someone in some way, then all we had to do was pay attention and tune in.

That's truly all it takes.

He struggled, struggled for so long I worried that he wouldn't hold out. But I kept my promise, and other than watching as the battle continued to wage, I didn't intrude. I just kept to myself as he experienced her entire emotional journey—her fear when her boys didn't return—her

overwhelming grief when she learned they never would—
her indignation when she found herself accused—her grim
acceptance when she was so unfairly tried—including the moment she gave up on herself—which happened to be the same
moment everyone else seemed to give up on her too. Even
though she knew she was innocent of their deaths, she still
found a place for the blame. She still chose to keep up her
punishment long after she'd already been hanged. And even
though her sons continued their existence in the very same
house, enjoying century after century of naughty, mischie-
vous pranks, it's like they were all so immersed in their own
separate worlds, they were completely unaware of each other.

"She's back," I whispered, knowing it to be true. "They're
all back together again. It's over, at last. Thanks to *you*."

I squeezed Bodhi's arm, my shoulders lifting when he
began to blink and stir. Bringing his hands to his face and rubbing his eyes before he squinted at me and said, "You okay?"

I nodded, far too choked up to trust my own voice. Instead thinking: *You?* Knowing he could hear it just as well as
any words I might speak.

He stretched his legs out before him, craned his neck
from side to side, arched his back for a moment, then stood.
Offering his hand as he pulled me up too, his entire expression changing when he said, "I told you not to interfere."

I balked, hardly believing what I'd just heard.

"I told you to stay out of it. But *nooo*, you wouldn't listen. You never listen. You have serious issues with listening." He shook his head, adding, "And the truth is, I'm not sure what to do with you, Riley. I'm not sure if I'm even the right guide for you. I mean, it's pretty obvious how hard it is for you to even *try* to respect me."

"*Wha*—" I shook my head, so many arguments rushing forth at once, I didn't know where to begin. "Are you *kidding* me?" I looked at him, one quick look and I knew he was most certainly not joking, not in the least. "Because for your information, I did what you asked, and let me just tell you it wasn't *at all* easy. In case you don't realize it. *I'm* the one who watched you go all weird and spasmy and freaky. All the while having no idea whatsoever whether or not you'd make it, not to mention what might possibly become of *me* if you didn't. And yet, I still just ignored my doubts, gulped down my fears, and kept treading water, not assisting you in any way, shape, or form. And then, even after I was spit out of there, even after you swallowed her grief and she twirled her way into the sky, all I did was touch your arm and make sure you were okay. That's it. I *swear.* So you have no right to say what you did. No right at all, in fact—"

He looked right at me, cutting in when he said, "See? That's exactly the kind of thing I'm talking about. Look at the way you speak to me! Tell me, Riley, were you like that when you were alive too? Did you talk that way to your parents, and your teachers in school?"

I screwed my lips to the side, placed my hands on my hips, and thought about it. Thought about it long and hard before saying, "Sometimes, yeah. What of it?"

He turned away, straightening his clothes and tucking the tail of his shirt back into his pants as he gazed out that small, square window and said, "The fact is, you *did* interfere. And now, because of it, I've no idea if I'll get the credit I so desperately need for moving her across the bridge." He shook his head and pinched the bridge of his nose, pausing for a few moments, collecting his thoughts, before he plunged ahead. "You have no idea what you've done. You don't have the first clue as to how this all works. You just jump right in, assuming you know way more than you do, refusing to pay any attention to what I've asked of you." He turned toward me, pushing a lock of wet hair off his face and back behind his ear when he said, "I probably shouldn't tell you this, because you'll just disrespect me that much more, but the Wailing Woman? She was my last chance. My last shot at redeeming myself and moving on. But now that you've butted in, despite my warning you to stay put, I'll probably get demoted, and that's if I'm lucky—"

"But that's the thing, I *didn't* interfere," I said, arms flailing through the air, desperate for him to believe it. "*That's* what I've been trying to tell you this whole entire time. *That's* what

you don't seem to get. I was there, yeah, we both know that. I saw the whole, entire thing. But that's *it*. All I did was *hope* and try to surround you with *hope*. I *hoped* that you'd realize your own inner strength. I *hoped* that you'd stay on course, on your mission to help her move on to a better place. That's *it*! I swear. So tell me, oh mighty guide, since when is *hope* considered a bad thing? Since when does *hope* get a person demoted? I mean, seriously, sheesh!" I shook my head and circled my arms high on my chest, dismayed once again at how easily they fit there. "If that's the way things work in the Here & Now, if they've truly got some kind of anti-*hope* campaign going on, then no thanks. I will *not* be returning anytime soon, no matter how many clever Soul Catchers they send after me. And I won't let Buttercup go back either. I'd rather we just stay right here and take over as the new ghosts of Warmington Castle. All I'd have to do is come up with some kind of cool, new, ghostly type gimmick that hasn't been done before and——" I sighed, running out of steam and shaking my head as my eyes met Bodhi's.

"You swear you didn't interfere?" he said, obviously wanting to believe.

"*Yes!*" I practically shouted, desperate for him to hear me. "I absolutely, positively, swear upon my very own grave!"

"Yes, but do you swear on your favorite Kelly Clarkson song?" He tilted his head and eyeballed me.

I gaped, wondering how he could've possibly known about my penchant for filling my iPod with all of her songs. Then just like that, I got it. He'd seen my footage. It was part of his prep work, before taking on the responsibility of me. He'd been forced to watch the whole lame saga of my life, the one that was unfortunately titled: *The (Short, Pathetic, Completely Wasted) Life of Riley—Everything You Ever Wanted to Know, from A to Z.*

"Don't worry, it wasn't the A to Z version," he said. "Just the highlights, the movie trailer version, that's all. But more importantly, are you saying I seriously did that—swallowed her grief and moved her toward the bridge all on my own?"

"Yeah." I nodded, seeing his face light up in a smile for the first time since I'd met him, and amazed by the way it completely transformed him. "Like I said, the only thing I offered was *hope*, nothing more. And they can't fault a person for *hope*, can they?"

He looked at me, still smiling when he said, "Nope, they most certainly can't." Leading Buttercup and me out of that room and glancing over his shoulder as he added, "So, what do you think? You still up for that flying lesson?"

## 22

Here's the thing—even after I'd mastered the art of being successfully airborne, neither of us had any idea what to do about a little problem named Buttercup.

Since we couldn't speak canine, and didn't know the first thing about how to go about reading his mind, well, let's just say we were totally and completely flummoxed as to how to get him off the ground.

Like everything else in my world, learning to fly all came down to one thing:

*Desire.*

Everything ran on desire.

Nothing was exempt.

Which meant no wings were necessary.

(Though some people happened to like the way they looked so much they wore them anyway. Which is how, according to Bodhi, that whole angel-with-wings thing got started.)

But still, in the end, it all came down to just how badly you wanted something.

Just how well you could imagine yourself having it and/or doing it.

And just how much you believed you truly could have it and/or do it.

It was simple.

Easy peasy.

All you had to do was know how to manifest it.

But the question was: *Could a dog actually manifest something?*

Something as foreign to them as flying would be?

And almost more importantly, why would Buttercup even *want* to pretend he was a bird gliding from tree branch to tree branch, when he so clearly loved being a dog?

But then, when I thought about it, really thought long and hard about it, I remembered the growing number of times I'd found him in his own little self-made nirvana—surrounded by piles of his favorite brand of doggie biscuits as he napped in a solitary warm patch of sun that hadn't been there a few moments earlier.

And at that moment I knew just what it would take to get him to take flight.

All we had to do was find a way to make Buttercup *want* to fly.

Otherwise, one of us was going to have to carry him all the way to London.

We were in one of the many gardens of Warmington Castle, having decided to use the one with the maze and the tangle of roses as a sort of runway. Even though I'd warned Bodhi that if I failed to launch, and ended up all snarled up in those sharp, thorny rosebushes instead, he'd never hear the end of it.

But he just laughed, that good-natured, wonderful tinkling sound of a laugh he'd definitely held firmly in check just a little while before, but after releasing the Wailing Woman, he seemed to use freely.

I guess his fear of failure, of possibly being demoted and all, is what made him so grumpy and serious. And, after he explained it to me, well, it seemed he had good reason.

That wasn't his first go-round with the Wailing Woman. He'd been there before.

Went with his own guide, who, by the way, he still firmly refuses to either name or describe but who he swears I'll get to meet someday—*maybe* (he put major emphasis on the *maybe*)—*if and when* (again, emphasis) he feels that I've earned it. Though he totally failed to elaborate on just how I might go about doing that.

But anyway, the way he told it, the first time he approached her, he took one look into those horrible, bottomless eyes of hers and hotfooted right down the stairs, through the corridor, down the other stairs, and bippidy blah blah, until he found his way outside in the garden, white as a sheet, and gasping for dear life (yep, even though he was already dead).

The second time, he knew he could not possibly behave like that again, not if he ever wanted to get his "glow on" (a term he also put great emphasis on, yet even though I pressed him, he completely refused to explain it to me), and so, when she turned and met his gaze, he didn't hold back even though he really, really wanted to.

He also didn't scream and go running out of that room.

Instead, he just dove right in, determined to swallow her grief and prove he could do it.

But, as soon as he started, he was so overwhelmed by her unending despair, he just spit it right back out at her, watching it drip and cling until she was able to absorb it back in.

And just after that, he was marched (so to speak) right back to the Here & Now where he was urged to enroll in some advanced classes on tolerance and compassion, where he finally grew and learned enough to graduate from his level, and move on to a higher level, where he was then urged to take on the not-so-easy task of guiding a spunky, snappy, snarky, slightly rebellious (his words, not mine) twelve-year-old girl who'd recently had her life ripped right out from under her.

Then when (not to mention *if!*) he gets a good handle on me, well, they told him that maybe, they just might consider letting him go for round three in the match of Bodhi versus the Wailing Woman.

All of which means we weren't even supposed to *be* at Warmington Castle in the first place.

Apparently there was an entirely different ghost all picked out and ready for me to, er, coax and convince its way to the bridge.

But, as Bodhi pointed out, as soon as he laid eyes on me, as soon as I took one look at him and deemed him dorky guy, well that's when he knew I could handle the Radiant Boy—or *Boys*, as it turned out.

And if, in the end, I couldn't, he figured I'd have the perfect opportunity to help myself to a nice big slice of the humble pie he claimed I so sorely deserved.

So yeah, maybe we were both feeling a little happy with ourselves.

A little "chuffed" as they say in jolly old England.

But why wouldn't we?

We'd just accomplished what those in charge, namely the members of the Council, were pretty much sure that we couldn't.

We'd both greatly succeeded, where a whole host of others had failed.

And all we were left with was the deceptively simple task of getting my sweet yellow Lab off the ground so we could go celebrate our mutual success in London.

But the thing about Buttercup is, no matter how cute and sweet and well behaved he might be, he's also kind of a wuss (as evidenced by the way he ran from the Radiant Boy, leaving me alone to defend myself).

Not to mention how he's kind of lazy too.

Because when Bodhi had the (what I thought at the time to be brilliant) idea of tossing his favorite brand of dog biscuits into the air in an attempt to convince him to soar after them, Buttercup just licked his chops, closed his eyes, and manifested his own pile of dog biscuits without so much as moving an inch.

So after several test runs of me soaring around the garden, buzzing my way through the maze with my hair streaming behind me and the wind howling at my cheeks, as Buttercup chased underneath me, barking and tail wagging like crazy—I realized something else about Buttercup.

He's domesticated.

A bona fide companion animal.

And what he hates more than anything in the world is to be left on his own for too long.

So when I called for Bodhi to join me, urging him to soar alongside me as we headed straight toward London without once looking back, to commit so fully to the mission that Buttercup would think we were never planning to return—he agreed.

Our reasoning being that there was only one way for him to join us on our trip, and that was for him to fly right alongside us.

There would be no carrying allowed.

So, we took off.

Both of us getting a good running start (not because it was necessary, but because it was fun).

Both of us flying side by side and doing our best not to look down as Buttercup chased along underneath us, sure it was some kind of game.

Both of us fully resolved to keep going, to not take a single look back, long after we'd flown over the large perimeter wall that for some strange reason stopped poor Buttercup right there in his tracks, until, just like me facing the Radiant Boys at their scariest, he realized his fear was all in his head and he ran through that too.

Both of us committed to just keep on keeping on—to not cave in to Buttercup's awful, unceasing, continuous series of forlorn whining, howling, and yelps as he chased underneath us. So sure he'd been dealt a cruel hand of fate, that he'd been permanently and completely abandoned to the ground.

Both of us waiting, *hoping* for Buttercup's desire to finally kick in just enough to where he'd be magically boosted and propelled right alongside us.

And just when I was sure I couldn't take it anymore, just as I was about to break my own promise and swoop down toward my poor frantic dog and scoop him into my arms—

I saw him.

Ears pinned close to his head as his tail wagged like crazy. Causing him to swoop and swerve and even dive-bomb a few times in a way that truly sent my insides spinning, until he figured it out, got ahold of himself, and learned to use it as a rudder, steering him along, and keeping him on course, until he was fully caught up and soaring right there alongside us, as though he'd been doing it for days.

And even though I couldn't listen in on his thoughts or read what might've been going on in his mind, his expression was all I needed to know that he loved every last second of it.

Loved it more than a warm patch of sun, a bowl full of biscuits, and an extra long car ride with all the windows rolled down.

Loved it more than all of those things combined.

Buttercup had found a new favorite pastime.

And he took to it as naturally and gracefully as a bird.

## 23

We soared through white, fluffy, mist-laden clouds.

We soared over snowy mountaintops and buildings and rivers and lakes.

We soared past large flocks of birds that Buttercup barked at and chased after, determined to get ahold of one and bring it back proudly as some kind of trophy in the way that he often did when he was alive. Each time glancing back at Bodhi and me in complete and utter confusion, when instead of capturing one of them, he flew directly *through* them.

And the moment we got to London, I *knew*.

Bodhi didn't have to tell me, didn't have to say a single word.

I just took one look at that wide winding river dotted with bridges and ships and lined with tall buildings, and I recognized it for exactly what it was.

The River Thames, the Westminster Bridge, Big Ben—we

flew over it all. We even swooped in really, really close to the topmost capsule on the London Eye, which, in case you don't know, is pretty much the earth plane's coolest Ferris wheel, then we swooped down toward the bottom and back up again, trailing it carefully as it went around and around in the sky.

And after that, we took to the streets, gliding above one of those bright-red double-decker buses London is famous for, and past brightly curtained windows of apartment buildings, or *flats* as the locals refer to them.

Then we swooped down even lower, just barely grazing the tops of tall trees, then lower still, just barely grazing the tops of tall people.

And when I extended my finger, just barely tapping the brim of some guy's hat and knocking it right off his bewildered head, Bodhi turned toward me, a disapproving look in his eyes as his lips sank down in a frown. But I just laughed and I stuck my tongue out at him before doing it again for good measure.

We kept going, heading toward a busy circle I thought I recognized from pictures I'd seen of Piccadilly, and that's when I spotted it.

Or rather, *them*.

The large crowds of people.

All of them hurrying off to the office, or school, or wherever

it is that people rush off to after eating their breakfast and getting dressed for the day.

All of them sharing one thing in common—they were all headed somewhere, and they were all determined to get there quickly.

All of those hundreds of people with somewhere to go—every last one of them totally and completely oblivious of me.

Having no clue that I soared right above them.

No idea that it was *I* who caused the stir on the backs of their necks and the breeze at their cheeks.

Completely unable to see me in the way I could see them.

Clearly.

Succinctly.

Down to every last detail.

They were alive and breathing and so utterly clear to me, and yet—not one of them had even the slightest sense we existed.

A girl, her guide, and her dog—all hovering right there above them.

Gazing upon the clueless masses beneath.

My throat grew all lumpy, and my eyes started to sting, so I forced myself to switch my attention to something else, watching as Buttercup continued to chase birds, looping and spinning and swirling and jumping, putting out increasing amounts of effort to no avail whatsoever, and coming no closer to understanding why he was so unsuccessful.

I even sneaked a peek at Bodhi, who'd ditched the nerd wear the moment we took flight, quick to explain how he thought the suited look would command more respect, make people (meaning me and his guide) take him more seriously than we would had he being wearing his usual gear. Though I think we could both agree that as far as experiments went, that particular one was a massive fail.

But having swapped out the nerd wear for the far more appropriate jeans and sweater and sneakers kids his age usually wear, he was about as far from a dorky guy as one could possibly get. And I guess that's why he seemed so *off* before. It was like, from the catcalls that followed him to the stage at graduation, to that casual, slouchy way that he stands, not to mention the way he really tears it up on a skateboard—well, it just didn't fit with the look he was trying to pull. It's like he was in disguise before, like he was wearing some kind of costume, determined to hide the fact that he was just like any other normal fourteen-year-old boy.

Only Bodhi wasn't normal.

Not even close.

Because not only was he dead. Not only was he my guide. But with his hair no longer greased back, with his clothes no longer coming from Nerd Central, with his face no longer

obscured by those awful, unbreakable frames that he wore, he was actually, well, *cute.*

No. Scratch that. Because the truth is, he was way past cute.

He was pretty much the Zac Efron of the afterlife.

But the second he caught my eye, caught me looking at him, I looked away.

The last thing I needed was for him to read those particular thoughts.

And just to protect myself further, just to keep everything orderly and straight and tucked away in its place, I'd also decided that, no matter how cute and nice he might continue to reveal himself to be—he would always, secretly at least, remain dorky guy to me.

It was easier that way.

I pushed my legs together and pointed my toes like arrows, having learned earlier that doing so would rid me of any and all wind resistance, and allow me to soar even faster and higher. And even though I heard Buttercup barking behind me, torn between chasing after me and a whole new flock of birds he'd stumbled upon, even though Bodhi called out to me, saying, "Hey—Riley—just say the word when you're ready to come in for a landing!" I pretended not to hear.

Because the truth is, after seeing all that I had, I could no longer find it within me to land.

I'd suddenly become aware of something I'd failed to see before.

The earth kept spinning.

People kept loving, and laughing, and breathing.

Everyone remained busy with the busy-making business of living.

And not one of them even sensed my existence.

Not one of them even knew I still walked among them.

Not to mention how it was time to face the fact that even the people who had known me—my friends and teachers and stuff—well, they'd already moved on. Already moved away from me, and on with their own lives—having reduced me to a small, packed-away memory of a poor, unfortunate, twelve-year-old girl whose life was abruptly cut short. Not wanting to dwell on my loss any longer than necessary, lest it make them ponder their own ever-shrinking existences.

And while I knew Ever missed me, as did my aunt Sabine, as far as everyone else was concerned, well, the number of people who even still thought of me on the rarest occasion was dwindling down to only a few.

I closed my eyes tightly, feeling that awful burn threatening to spill out the sides, as I took a moment to quickly list all of the very good and valid reasons why I had absolutely no plausible motive to cry.

1. I felt more alive than ever, despite my current state of invisibility.
2. I had just completed my task, Bodhi completed his, and the two of us together had truly helped our fellow souls and done something good.
3. I was flying! Soaring over a part of the world I'd always wanted to see, and to make it even better, my dog was sailing and swooping through the clouds right along with me.
4. My guide turned out to be not nearly as big of a dork as I'd first pegged him to be, which also meant he might not be quite so horrible to work with in the future. Not to mention how I just might've learned a very important lesson about judging people based solely on their appearance.

Or maybe not.

That last bit would remain to be seen.

And just as I was thinking these things, my eyes still shut tightly, blocking everything out of my sight, Bodhi swooped up from behind me and yelled, "Hey, Riley—watch out!"

My eyes snapped open, only to find myself soaring head-on into a tall building made of the kind of glass that reflects everything around it.

And I was struck.

Not by fear, since I knew I was in no danger, I'd just simply sail right through it if I failed to stop or slow down.

No, the truth is, I was struck by *me.*

Struck by the *sight* of me.

By the way my whole body glowed in a way that it had never done before.

Glowed in the way cheerleader girl's had.

Glowed in a similar way to Bodhi's and everyone else's I saw on that stage.

And even though my glow wasn't anywhere near as bright as theirs—

I still shone.

There was no denying it.

I swerved to the right, narrowly avoiding crashing smack through my own image at the very last second, before swooping, making a big, loopy U-turn, and confronting myself once again.

Seeing it all laid out before me plain as day.

My smallish, slim body, my practically sunken, flat chest, my lank blond hair with the bangs that fell into bright blue eyes that flanked the beginnings of what swooped down to be an undeniably semi-stubby nose. But my cheeks were widened and flushed as a big toothy grin spread across my

face, as I continued to stare at the brilliant, pale greenish glow that shimmered and danced all around me.

"You see it?" Bodhi said, coming up right beside me, his smile almost as big as mine.

I nodded, so struck by my appearance, at first I couldn't speak. Having to clear my throat a bunch of times before I could utter, "Yeah, I see it. But what does it mean?" Glancing at him briefly before focusing back on this sparkling new version of me.

"It means you got your *glow on*." He smiled, hovering right there alongside me. "It means you're on your way."

# 24

E ven though I initially wanted to stop, and maybe even pick up some souvenirs for my family (still don't know how I would've handled the actual logistics of that, but it seemed like a good idea at the time), after seeing my glowing reflection, after listening to Bodhi explain that there are many different levels to the Here & Now, and how each one just gets better and better than the one just before it, and how my new pale-green glow clearly marked me as a bona fide member of the level 1.5 team, and that if I kept up the good work, I'd be transcending that color and level in no time at all, going on to glow in a variety of colors, each of them representing a higher and higher sphere—after he explained all of that, I no longer felt the need to land.

London was a busy city.

Too busy for me.

And to be honest, I'd grown pretty weary of the spying life anyway.

Of existing vicariously through the living.

Especially now that I was finally clued in to the irony of it all—of how my life would only get richer and richer even though to all those below I was buried and dead.

But more importantly, for the first time in a long time, I had somewhere important to be.

For the first time in a long time, I had no need to live through someone else's experiences. Not when it was so clearly time to start claiming my own.

"Let's head back," I said, at first a little shaken by my decision, though it was soon overruled by eager anticipation. Knowing I'd be back to visit the earth plane again, sooner rather than later considering how many more ghosts it was my job to cross over, but for now, I just wanted to celebrate my victory in the one place in which I truly belonged. "Let's just go *home*." I smiled, soaring ahead and instinctively knowing just how to get there.

Occasionally gazing down at the earth plane as I soared through the clouds, knowing that just like all of the people rushing around right below me, I too had somewhere important to be.

# Coming in Spring 2011

*Riley's, Buttercup's, and Bodhi's*
*adventures continue in*
Shimmer

"Go on, Buttercup—go get it, boy!"

I cupped my hands around my mouth and squinted into a blanket of gooey, white haze still hours away from being burned off by the sun. Gazing upon a beach that was just the way I liked it—foggy, cold, a tiny bit spooky even. Reminding me of our old family visits to the Oregon Coast— the kind I sometimes tried to re-create on my own.

But despite the infinite manifesting possibilities of the Here & Now, something about it just wasn't the same. Sure you could replicate the same sensations, the way the tiny, pebbly grains wedged between your toes, the way the cool ocean spray felt upon your face, but still, it didn't quite cut it.

Couldn't quite live up to the real thing.

And clearly Buttercup agreed.

He sprinted after the stick, running headfirst into a dad enjoying an early morning stroll with his son, before emerging on their other side. Causing the kid to stop and stare and gaze all around—sensing the disturbance, the sudden change in atmosphere, the burst of cold air—the usual signs a ghost is present.

The usual signs kids always tune into, and their parents always miss.

I shut my eyes tightly, concentrating on mingling my energy with my surroundings. Summoning the vibration of the sand—the seashells—even the haze—longing to experience it in the same way I used to, knowing I'd have only a few moments of this before Buttercup returned, dropped the wet, slobbery stick at my feet, and we repeated the sequence again.

He was tireless. True to his breed, he'd happily *retrieve* for hours on end. A nice, long game of fetch making the list of his top five favorite things, ranking right up there with dog biscuits, a warm patch of sun, bird chasing, and, of course, his newest love—*flying*.

Nudging my leg with his nose, letting me know he was back, he stared up at me with those big brown eyes, practically begging me to hurl the stick even farther this time.

So I did.

Watching as it soared high into the sky before it pierced the filmy, white veil and was gone. Buttercup dashing behind it, tongue lolling out the side of his mouth, tail wagging crazily from side to side—the furry, yellow tip the last thing I saw before the mist swallowed him whole and he vanished from sight. Leaving only a faint echo of excited barks trailing behind.

I turned my attention to the small flock of seagulls circling overhead, swooping toward the water and filling their beaks with unsuspecting fish, before taking flight again. Vaguely aware of the minutes slipping past with still no sign of him, I called out his name, then chased it with a spot-on imitation of my dad's special whistle that never failed to bring Buttercup home. My feet carving into the sand, leaving no trace of footprints, as I pushed through a fog so thick, so viscous, it reminded me of the time I'd flown through a cloud storm for fun, only to realize it was anything but. And I was just about to venture into the freezing cold water, knowing of his fondness for swimming, when I heard a deep, unmistakable growl that immediately set me on edge.

Buttercup rarely growled.

He was far too good-natured for that.

So when he did, it was safe to assume he'd stumbled upon something serious.

Something very, very bad.

I followed the sound of it. That low, gravelly rumble growing in intensity the closer I crept. Only to be replaced with something much worse—a horrible snarl, a high-pitched yelp, and a sickening silence that made my gut dance.

"Buttercup?" I called, my voice so shaky, so unsteady I was forced to clear my throat and try again. "Buttercup— *where are you*? This isn't funny, you know! You better show yourself, *now*, or you will *not* be flying home!"

The second the threat was out, I heard him. Paws beating against the hard, wet sand, his quick, panting breath getting louder and louder the closer he ran.

I sighed in relief and sank down to the ground. Readying myself for the big, slobbery, apology hug that soon would be mine, only to watch in absolute horror as the fog split wide-open and a large dog jumped out.

A dog that *wasn't* Buttercup.

It was—*something else entirely.*

Big—the size of a pony.

Black—its coat matted and gnarled.

With paws the size of hooves that came hurtling toward me, as I screamed long and loud, desperate to get out of its way.

But it was too late.

No matter how fast I moved—it wasn't fast enough.

There was no escaping the chains of its sharply barbed collar that clanged ominously.

No escaping the menacing glow of those deep yellow eyes with the laser-hot gaze that burned right into mine, right into my soul . . .

# acknowledgments

Big, huge, glittery thanks to all the fabulous people at St. Martin's Press and Macmillan Children's who help bring my stories to life, including, but not limited to, Matthew Shear, Rose Hilliard, Anne Marie Tallberg, Katy Hershberger, Brittney Kleinfelter, Angela Goddard, Jean Feiwel, and Jennifer Doerr.

To Bill Contardi—agent extraordinaire!

To Sandy—who reads everything first!

And, of course, a very special thanks to my readers, for all of your warmth and humor and generous support. You make me feel like the luckiest author in the world!

# Questions for the Author

*In what ways are you similar (or different) to Riley Bloom?*

Actually, Riley and I share a lot in common. I know what it's like to be the baby of the family, and though I hate to admit it, I've also been known to hog the microphone while playing Rock Band on the Wii!

*How do you come up with your characters?*

Honestly, I'm not really sure! The story idea usually comes first, and then as I'm busy working on all the ins and outs of the new world I'm creating, the cast just sort of appears.

*What was your inspiration for the "Here & Now," the magical realm where Riley lives?*

Back when I first started working on The Immortals series, I did quite a bit of research on metaphysics, quantum physics, ghosts, spirits, and the afterlife, etc, all of which sort of fed into the concept of the "Here & Now." I guess, in a way, it's how I hope the afterlife will be.

*Do you believe in ghosts?*

In a word—yes. I've definitely experienced enough unexplainable phenomena to ever rule it out.

*If a ghost tried to scare you with your own worst fears (the way the Radiant Boys try to scare Riley), what fears might they use against you?*

I definitely drew upon all of my own worst fears while writing that scene—a crazy snake-haired clown wielding dental instruments is about as bad as it gets for me! The only thing missing was a really high ledge with no railing (I have a major fear of heights), but I wasn't sure how to fit that into the context, so I spared Riley that.

*Did you grow up with an older sister the way Riley did? How many brothers and sisters do you have?*

I have two older sisters, both of whom I completely idolized. There's a bit of an age gap between us, one is ten years older, and the other five years older, and trust me when I say that I did my best to emulate them. I listened to their music, watched their TV shows, and read their books—all of which was way more appealing than my own, more age-appropriate stuff. And like Riley, I used to try on their clothes and makeup when they were out with their friends, though I suspect that revelation will come as no surprise to them!

### Where do you write your books?

I have a home office where I put in very, very long hours seven days a week—but I have the best job in the world, so I'm not complaining!

### Have you always wanted to be a writer?

Well, first, I wanted to be a mermaid, and then a princess, but ever since sixth grade when I finished reading my first Judy Blume book, *Are You There God? It's Me, Margaret*, I decided I'd rather write instead. I'd always been an avid reader, but Judy Blume's books were some of the first that I could directly relate to, and I knew then that someday I wanted to try to write like that too.

### What would you do if you ever stopped writing?

Oh, I shudder to even think about it. I truly can't imagine a life without writing. Though I suppose I'd probably start traveling more. I've traveled a good bit already, both when I was working as a flight attendant and just on my own, but there are still so many places left to explore—oh, and I'd probably enroll in some art classes too—painting, jewelry making—crafty stuff like that.

### What would your readers be most surprised to learn about you?

Not long ago, every time I finished writing a book I would celebrate by cleaning my house, which, I have to say, was sorely in need of it by then. But recently, I've come to realize just how very sad and pathetic that is, so now I get a pedicure instead (and save the housecleaning for another day)!

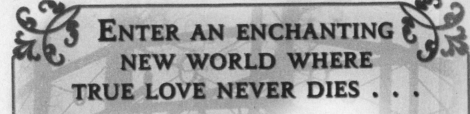

# ENTER AN ENCHANTING NEW WORLD WHERE TRUE LOVE NEVER DIES . . .

While Riley's learning how to make her way in the afterlife, her older sister Ever is learning what it's like to be immortal back on Earth.

ISBN: 978-0-312-53275-8
$9.95 US / $10.95 Can

ISBN: 978-0-312-53276-5
$9.99 US / $12.75 Can

ISBN: 978-0-312-65005-6
$9.99 US / $11.99 Can

ISBN: 978-0-312-59097-0
$17.99 US / $19.99 Can

For free downloads, hidden surprises, and glimpses into the future visit www.ImmortalsSeries.com

 St. Martin's Griffin

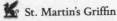